"You're a good man."

He ran his fingers through his hair and shook his head. Dark intensity pushed through the cool look in his eyes and hinted at a pain deep inside. "There are things you don't know, Kate."

"There are things I do know, Joe." She put her hand on his arm and saw something flicker in his expression. "I was wrong not to trust you with J.T. I won't make that mistake again."

"So you're going to allow me to spend unsupervised time with my son?"

"As much as you want," she confirmed. "He deserves to know his father. Because you *are* a good man."

She started to walk away and felt his strong fingers on her wrist. When he tugged her into his arms, the heat in his eyes stole the air from her lungs.

"If I were a good man, I wouldn't have been thinking about this. Let alone do it in a hospital."

He lowered his head and captured her lips....

Dear Reader,

Have you ever wondered about the guy who made you contemplate happily-ever-after, but for whatever reason things didn't work out? What would you do if that man suddenly showed up on your doorstep?

In *When a Hero Comes Along,* this is the dilemma facing Kate Carpenter. Dashing Marine Corps helicopter pilot Joe Morgan abruptly broke things off with her before going overseas, then rekindles the relationship because of their baby. She never stopped caring about him, but his rejection hurt so very much she's determined not to go down that road again. Instead, for the sake of their child, they're forced to follow a different path—one that eventually leads to love.

When a Hero Comes Along is for all of us who remember the one who makes us sometimes think about what might have been. For me, that one was named Joe.

Enjoy!

Teresa Southwick

WHEN A HERO
COMES ALONG

TERESA SOUTHWICK

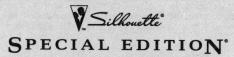

SPECIAL EDITION®

Published by Silhouette Books

America's Publisher of Contemporary Romance

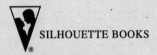

SILHOUETTE BOOKS
®

ISBN-13: 978-0-373-24904-6
ISBN-10:   0-373-24904-7

WHEN A HERO COMES ALONG

Copyright © 2008 by Teresa Ann Southwick

Printed in U.S.A.

Books by Teresa Southwick

Silhouette Special Edition

The Summer House #1510
   "Courting Cassandra"
*Midnight, Moonlight &
   Miracles* #1517
It Takes Three #1631
The Beauty Queen's Makeover #1699
At the Millionaire's Request #1769
§§*Paging Dr. Daddy* #1886
‡*The Millionaire and the M.D.* #1894
‡*When a Hero Comes Along* #1905

Silhouette Books

The Fortunes of Texas
   Shotgun Vows

Silhouette Romance

*Wedding Rings and
   Baby Things* #1209
The Bachelor's Baby #1233
A Vow, a Ring, a Baby Swing #1349
The Way to a Cowboy's Heart #1383
And Then He Kissed Me #1405
With a Little T.L.C. #1421
The Acquired Bride #1474
Secret Ingredient: Love #1495
The Last Marchetti Bachelor #1513
**Crazy for Lovin' You* #1529
**This Kiss* #1541
**If You Don't Know by Now* #1560
**What If We Fall in Love?* #1572
Sky Full of Promise #1624
†*To Catch a Sheik* #1674
†*To Kiss a Sheik* #1686
†*To Wed a Sheik* #1696

††*Baby, Oh Baby* #1704
††*Flirting with the Boss* #1708
††*An Heiress on His
   Doorstep* #1712
§*That Touch of Pink* #1799
§*In Good Company* #1807
§*Something's Gotta Give* #1815

*The Marchetti Family
**Destiny, Texas
†Desert Brides
††If Wishes Were…
§Buy-a-Guy
‡The Men of Mercy Medical
§§The Wilder Family

TERESA SOUTHWICK

lives with her husband in Las Vegas, the city that reinvents itself every day. An avid fan of romance novels, she is delighted to be living out her dream of writing for Silhouette Books.

To all the men and women in the U.S. military—
past and present.
Your service and sacrifice are deeply appreciated.

Chapter One

It wasn't every day a man had the chance to come back from the dead.

More to the point, Marine Captain Joe Morgan had come back from hell. He knew what it felt like to face off with a cold-eyed terrorist who hated his guts and was determined to kill him. He knew what he'd done to keep from being killed and that secret would go with him to his grave, where it belonged.

Now he had to face Kate Carpenter, although she probably hated his guts, too. She had good reason, but he still had to see her. And his baby boy. He had to explain.

And here he was on her doorstep.

He lifted a hand to knock, then curved his fingers into a fist. Maybe he should have called first, he thought, running his fingers through his hair. He wasn't one for putting things off. Mostly. Sooner or later they had to see each other. Although he'd been standing here for five minutes without knocking.

Glancing around the apartment complex, he didn't see anyone moving around.

The pathways through the rock-and-shrub landscaping were well-lit. He'd specifically timed this meeting for nineteen-thirty hours, seven-thirty at night, because it was early enough not to be too late, and late enough that he figured she'd be home. And with any luck not so late that she'd shut the door in his face.

But if he stood here much longer, anyone watching would wonder if he was up to no good. He probably was no good, enough to show up here anyway.

He ran a hand through his hair again, then pressed the doorbell, but he heard nothing and wondered if that was due to thick walls or a broken doorbell. Or was he broken? War was a noisy business; it took all kinds of tolls. Maybe his hearing had suffered.

But he'd passed his flight physical and could hardly wait to get back to the business of flying for his half of Southwestern Helicopter Service. The fact that his bastard of a brother owned the other half wasn't something he could think about now.

Inside the apartment a shadow passed the window and he heard light footsteps on the other side of the door. If Kate was as smart as he thought, she'd be peeking through the peephole. Assuming she could reach it. It had been fourteen months, but he hadn't forgotten how small and slender she was. He was six feet tall, yet she'd fitted perfectly against him, and the thought made him ache deep down inside.

Several moments passed and he realized his heart was racing. Between Afghanistan and Kate Carpenter, his ticker was getting a pretty good workout. But any second now the suspense would be over.

Any second.

Now.

He waited, but nothing happened. Was she standing there? Did she see him? What if she didn't open the door? Could he really blame her?

He really *should* have called first.

"Kate?" He knocked lightly on the door. "It's Joe. Morgan," he added. In case she didn't remember him.

He didn't think that was likely. Not after the letter and what she'd said in it. But he knew from personal experience that women could turn the right memories off when they wanted to do wrong.

Inside, a chain scraped just before the dead bolt clicked and Kate opened the door. She didn't say anything, just stared up at him, eyes wide, full lips parted slightly in shock. That was something he recognized. Shock was protection for mind and body—a time-out until the two were strong enough to handle trauma. He'd never actually thought of himself as a trauma. Not consciously. But now he realized he hadn't called because he was afraid she would hang up on him. Refuse to see or talk to him.

Now that she was close enough for him to feel the warmth of her skin, he knew how badly he'd *needed* to see and talk to her. She was even more beautiful than he remembered. Her eyes were huge and his memories hadn't done them justice. At first glance he'd call them brown. But a closer look showed flecks of gold, reminding him that when she looked into the sun her eyes turned almost green. She was still small, and with clothes on it was hard to tell, but he would swear she was curvier than the last time he'd held her—made love to her.

Brown hair hung in shiny layers to her shoulders, and was still the same as when he'd run his fingers through it and kissed her until her breath was a sigh of surrender. Then her eyes had turned green and the sun had had nothing to do with it. But she wasn't smiling now and he longed to see the dimples he knew would magically appear when the corners of her mouth turned up.

"Kate?"

She gasped, as if his voice brought her out of shock. "Joe," she whispered. "I—I didn't think I'd ever see you again."

"Surprise." He shrugged, then hooked his thumbs in the pockets of his worn jeans and leaned against the doorjamb.

"What are you doing here?"

That wasn't what he'd expected, yet it provided his first clue that he'd had a script of this meeting. In his head there had been smiles, dimples, hugs and—if he was really lucky— maybe a tear or two—followed by a heartfelt declaration of how glad she was that he'd come home.

"I wanted to see you."

"Why?"

He wanted to think this was shock talking, but he knew better. She'd been hurt when he'd abruptly told her they were over. She hadn't understood that it was for the best and he hadn't explained why he felt that way.

"I got the letter," he said.

"I wasn't sure." Her chin lifted. "You didn't write back."

"There's a reason for that—"

"It doesn't matter." Her full lips pressed tightly together for a moment. "You made it clear that I was nothing more than a fling. We had fun. Just an affair."

A hot and steamy affair, he thought. Instant attraction that had burst into flame. They couldn't get enough of each other. But she was right. He had made it clear they were over, unfortunately, his memories were not. And one of his most vivid was of the last time he'd seen her, when she'd been wearing nothing more than a sheet and a pair of dimples. Then he'd dumped her and the dimples had disappeared.

"I remember what I said."

"Then you remember you told me not to bother waiting. That I shouldn't expect—"

"About expecting…" he said.

She looked down for a moment, then met his gaze. "I—I only wrote because I thought you had a right to know—"

This is where the whole right and wrong thing tweaked his tail rotor. "How soon did you know?"

Something like guilt flickered in her eyes. "What is it you're asking?"

"Whether you were going to tell me at all."

"I did have some conflict about that," she admitted. "I—"

"Can we discuss this inside?" He glanced at the apartment doors on either side of hers. "Let me go out on a limb here and point out that you probably don't want the neighbors eavesdropping on this conversation."

She caught her lip between her teeth and her expression told him she was seriously thinking about turning him down. Then she stepped back and pulled the door wide. "Okay. Come in."

Before she could change her mind, he walked inside. From where he stood he could see a kitchen and dining area with a French door that led to a small patio. The walls were painted light gold with white crown molding and six-paneled doors. Neutral beige carpet. But the painting of wine bottles and the decorative wrought-iron plate rack personified Kate. It was cute and charming and colorful.

He turned and looked down at her. In her snug jeans and a scoop-necked T-shirt that hugged every curve, she almost made him forget that he wanted to know why she'd waited so long to tell him she was pregnant. If he'd found out sooner, would it have changed things? That's something he would never know.

"About the letter," he said.

"We hardly knew each other, Joe. You made it clear you didn't want to be tied down. And why would you believe I wasn't trying to trap you?"

"Before I get blamed for something, shouldn't I get a chance to screw up first?"

"And didn't I have a right to know that you only wanted sex? Somehow I missed the signs." Her eyes flashed a color that was new to him. "For the record, I don't blame you. No one held a gun to my head."

That's for sure. She'd been warm and willing in his arms. And he'd wanted her more every time he saw her. Even after all this time, he still wanted her. "I was there. I'm back now." Maybe he was the one blaming her when she hadn't screwed up.

But he'd been fooled once and that was enough. Maybe the experience had fine-tuned his cheater meter, because he believed her. "He's my son, too."

In a split second, the expression on her face went from woman scorned to mother lion. "Since when? You made it clear that you didn't want to participate when you didn't write back."

He shook his head. "I didn't write back because I couldn't."

"Oh? Your arms were broken?" She sighed and shook her head. "That was a cheap shot. Look, Joe, the fact is I don't want or need anything from you. I felt obligated to let you know about the baby. You didn't—*couldn't* write back. End of story."

"Not so fast. I'm here now." He'd have been here sooner if not for mission debriefing, medical clearance and military retirement paperwork. And this conversation wasn't one he'd wanted to have over the phone. Or in front of her neighbors. Or, apparently, sitting down on the sofa. He met her accusing gaze. "There is an explanation. And I'd like you to hear me out."

"Okay." She folded her arms over her breasts and stared him straight in the eye.

"The letter arrived just as I was getting ready for a mission and I was going to answer it when I got back."

"I see."

"The thing is—it took me some time to get back."

"What?" There was a wary look in her eyes. "Why?"

"My helicopter was shot down and the Taliban extended their hospitality for a while."

And that was all she needed to know, all he would tell her.

Her eyes went from dark brown back to warm cocoa as she put her hand on his arm. "Joe—"

The touch of her fingers felt too good and he backed up a step. "I got in a little while ago and came straight from McCarran."

That was important for her to know.

"I don't know what to say," she said.

"Tell me about my son."

A smile curved up the corners of her mouth. "He's perfect, the best thing I've ever done."

"What's his—what did you name him?"

She walked over to the end table beside the sofa and picked up a framed photo, then handed it to him. "J.T."

As Joe stared at the chubby-faced infant in the picture something inside him went tight and his heart skipped. The baby's eyes were big, blue like his own, but he had his mother's dimples. "What does J.T. stand for?"

She hesitated a moment, then said, "Joseph Turner—that was my grandfather's name."

He slid his gaze to hers and grinned. "Has a nice ring."

"I thought so." She shrugged.

"He's about four months old?"

She nodded and his gaze lowered to Kate's now-flat abdomen. He wondered what she'd looked like pregnant. "Can I see him?"

"He's asleep," she said quickly, protectively.

"I just want to see him."

She thought about that for too long and frowned while she was at it. Finally, she nodded. "This way."

He followed her into the baby's room. A night-light kept it from being too dark and he could see the crib, some kind of box overflowing with toys and a changing table. There were stuffed animals everywhere. Slowly, he walked over and stared down at the child, peacefully sleeping on his back. His small mouth pursed and worked in a sucking movement, then a little sigh escaped. His chest had felt tight many times before, but this was a sensation he'd never before experienced.

Joe reached out a finger and touched one tiny fist. He had to clear the lump in his throat before he could state the obvious, "He's so little."

A tender expression softened her face. "You should have seen him when he was born."

But he hadn't, although that wasn't her fault. For six months he hadn't even known there was going to be a baby and that *was* her fault. He hadn't been there while his child grew inside her, or when she went into labor and gave birth. She'd robbed him of the beginning and an enemy on the other side of the world had stolen the rest. What if an attack of conscience hadn't forced her to let him know? In his experience women kept a lot of things to themselves and none of it was in his best interest.

He met her gaze. "We need to talk."

"Agreed. But not here and not tonight. Call me tomorrow?"

Sounded like an evasive maneuver to him. To fly choppers in a war theater, Joe had trained to run and dive to stay alive. But good training went hand in hand with tactics. Surprise was the best strategy.

"All right," he said. "You'll hear from me tomorrow."

* * *

Near Mercy Medical's emergency entrance Kate Carpenter stood about twenty yards from the square concrete slab with the big red *X* in the center of a circle marked with a blue *H*. This was where the medical evacuation helicopters landed. One was on its way with a fifty-eight-year-old male. Possible heart attack. The patient was from Pahrump. Because her mother lived there, she knew it was an hour from Las Vegas on a winding two-lane road. Medical intervention would have taken too long if he'd been brought in by regular ambulance.

Mercy Medical Center E.R. nurses alternated meeting the medevac chopper and today was Kate's turn. The emergency-room doctor had already seen the EKG strip and was keeping in touch with the situation via radio and the readings from the heart monitor hooked up to the patient. This was a level-three trauma center, and it was where she'd met Joe Morgan for the first time. Talk about trauma.

She still couldn't believe he'd shown up last night without warning. Not that a warning would have helped her on the inside, but her outside would have looked a lot better. At least she could have put on lip gloss and mascara. A woman shouldn't have to meet *the* man from her past without benefit of cosmetics.

She'd half expected to see him when the calendar said his twelve months overseas were over. But one day had turned into another and time had passed without any word from Joe. Finally, she'd figured he was one of those guys who was nothing more than a sperm donor. The look on his face when he'd seen his son for the first time told her she'd been wrong. That worried her more, even though he'd never asked to hold J.T.

Her emotional reserves had been about depleted when she'd finally suggested they meet another time to discuss the situation. He'd agreed, then left, looking tired. He was a little leaner than when she'd last seen him and she wondered what he'd been through. His cavalier explanation about the Taliban extending their hospitality wasn't much information, but she had her suspicions—and a very bad feeling. He might be leaner and meaner, but he still packed that Morgan punch that kicked her pulse, heart rate and respiration into the danger zone.

Then she heard the whump, whump of helicopter blades growing louder and looked up as the bird seemed to float closer. When the rotor wash was near enough to blow her hair off her face, she gave herself a mental pinch to get her mind off personal problems and into the trauma.

She waited impatiently until the blades stopped moving, then ducked her head and with the respiratory therapist moved the gurney to the open door of the chopper. The flight nurse helped them offload the patient and handed over Jim Bennett's paperwork, then they wheeled him to treatment room six in the E.R.

After transferring him to the exam table, Kate wrapped the blood-pressure cuff on his upper arm. "I'm going to get your vitals, Mr. Bennett."

"Okay." The man had a full head of brown hair streaked with silver and the pallor of his face reflected his pain and fear.

She removed the stethoscope from around her neck and plugged it into her ears, then put the bell in the bend of his arm and pumped up the cuff. After listening carefully, she noted the results. Next came pulse and respirations which she also marked on his chart. She was giving the patient a couple of aspirin when Dr. Mitch Tenney walked into the room.

The doctor took the chart from her and flipped through it. Without looking at the patient, he said, "Mr. Bennett, you're having an M.I."

"What's that?" The man's fearful gaze moved back and forth between them. His anxiety quotient was edging him toward panic.

"Myocardial infarction," Mitch said.

"Heart attack," Kate translated.

"We're going to give you some anticoagulants, a clot buster and some morphine for the pain." Mitch looked at her. "Per my standing orders."

"Okay," she said nodding.

"Then we're going to transfer you upstairs to the cardiac-care unit for observation." Mitch started to walk out.

"Am I going to die?" Mr. Bennett asked.

Mitch finally looked at him. "Not today."

Kate shook her head at the doctor's curtness. Mitch Tenney was the finest trauma specialist she'd ever seen. What he lacked in bedside manner he made up for in skill. And that's probably the only reason he was still on staff. Mercy Medical administration had received more than one complaint and the doctor was flirting with his third strike.

She stayed with the patient until he was transferred upstairs, then checked in at the nurse's station. "If I'm all clear, I'm going to grab some lunch."

The supervisor looked up from her computer monitor. "Go, Kate. It's late. You must be starving."

"Yeah. Been one of those mornings."

And it got just a little more unpredictable when she walked through the waiting room on her way to the cafeteria. Joe stood there dressed in a khaki flight suit, aviator sunglasses hanging from the V where his white T-shirt peeked above the zipper.

"Hi," he said.

"What are you doing here?"

Mentally she smacked her forehead. He wasn't dressed up for Halloween. These were work clothes for a helicopter pilot.

She just hadn't connected the right dots fast enough to realize that he was *her* helicopter pilot. He'd brought Mr. Bennett in.

"Scratch that," she said, shaking her head. She wasn't prepared to deal with him again so soon. Part of the reason she'd cut last night's visit short was to pull herself together, but one sleepless night of thinking about him hadn't been long enough to settle her traumatized nerves. And when he stood there looking like temptation for the taking, she knew her nerves wouldn't be upgraded from critical to stable any time soon. "I guess what I meant to say was don't you have somewhere else to be?"

"Not at the moment."

He looked good, she thought. The one-piece flight suit should look dorky, but didn't. Not on Joe. It was impossibly masculine, along with his short dark hair which was mussed in a good way. Dark-blue eyes met hers and he seemed more serious than she remembered. More compelling. And more dangerous.

He was still handsome, and looking at him did scary things to the rhythm of her heart, which had already worked pretty darn hard in less than twenty-four hours. But he was different somehow. The self-confident, cocky air that had first captured her interest was missing in action. He seemed more watchful, wary, on full alert.

His face was strong, with a square jaw and a nose that was not quite straight. Looking closer, she noticed a scar on his chin, a back-slash that she didn't recall. And she would. She'd kissed every inch of his face during those intense weeks they'd been together, before he'd abruptly told her it was over between them.

Kate slid her hands into the pockets of her scrubs as she looked up at him. "I'm on my way to lunch."

"Mind if I join you?"

She shrugged. "Suit yourself. But it's hospital food. Don't say I didn't warn you."

"Roger that."

The cafeteria was on the first floor and she led him through the maze of hallways until the scent of food drifted to them. It was late for lunch and the room was practically empty. They took red plastic trays from the stack and slid them along the metal shelf in front of the steam table while studying the day's menu choices—beef stroganoff and chicken teriyaki. She looked up at Joe, intending to break the tension and say something light and innocuous about the awful food, but her tongue refused to work. She was immobilized by the expression in his eyes—probing, intense, alive, knowing. Suddenly she wasn't hungry—at least not for food.

She cleared her throat, then said, "I recommend a hamburger."

He nodded, and she ordered two. They got drinks from the fountain dispenser, then filed by the cashier and Kate insisted on paying because of her employee discount.

When they were facing each other across a table, she cut her hamburger in half. Anything to keep her hands busy. Unfortunately, the movement also highlighted the fact that they were shaking. "So— I didn't expect to see you so soon."

"It was bound to happen."

"Because of J.T.," she said.

"Because Southwestern Helicopter Service is my company and we have the contract for medical evacuation with Mercy Medical Center."

"I knew that." It was another reason she'd half expected to see him when his tour of duty ended. "I just figured as owner of the company, you were running the show from behind a desk."

"No way." He shook his head. "The way I see it, anyone who doesn't want to fly is crazy."

Mentally she raised her hand for a free pass to the psych ward. She liked both feet on the ground, thank you very much. One irreconcilable difference in the con column and she suspected there would be more. Part of the problem was that she didn't know how many more. She'd spent several sizzling weeks with this man and talking hadn't been high on her list of things to do with him. But the list had changed. He was J.T.'s father and she knew very little about him, except that he'd charmed her into breaking her rules, then disappeared and broke her heart. That's what happened when you didn't follow the rules. She wouldn't be making that mistake again.

"I see," she said.

Without cutting it in half, he took a manly bite of his burger, then chewed. "So, who watches J.T. while you're at work?"

Probably he'd have asked that even if she hadn't mentioned their son a few moments ago. And she was going to cut him a break on the slightly judgmental tone in his voice and chalk it up to her imagination, aggravated by guilt from leaving her son in order to make a living and put a roof over his head. "I have someone."

"I guess you checked out this someone?"

"Of course. She's mature. A grandmother." When she noticed the look on his face, she added, "A young grandmother. She has references."

Joe finished his hamburger while she picked at hers and made crumbs out of the bun. Without consciously forming the thought, Kate had known that Joe showing up would complicate her life. But this conversation was making her uneasy. Somewhere she'd heard that the best defense was a good offense. Although whoever had said it probably wasn't facing off with an honest-to-goodness warrior.

"Look, Joe, I'm not sure exactly what you're getting at. But I've got questions, too. Like, why didn't you call before coming by last night?"

He shrugged. "I'm a fly-by-the-seat-of-the-pants kind of guy."

"And I'm a feet-on-the-ground and plan-everything-out kind of girl."

"Not when we were together," he said, heat blazing in his eyes.

He was right about that. From the time she was old enough to understand that her mother chose one loser after another, Kate had promised herself that she wouldn't make the same mistakes. She would do things in a practical, orderly way. She would fall in love, get married, and after a reasonable length of time, probably two years, they would have a baby.

Then she'd met Joe. He came into Mercy Medical's E.R. for stitches in his hand and laid his follow-me-into-sin grin on her. She'd known she was flirting with danger, but the excitement of it was irresistible. She couldn't believe that a man like him was interested in Candy Carpenter's only daughter and for once she silenced the practical voice that warned her to run far, run fast. Instead, she'd run straight into his arms for a magical month.

Then he'd simply said it was over and he was deploying for a year. After that, she'd buried her pain behind an it-serves-me-right attitude and figured she got off with a cheap lesson. Mostly she believed that until she found out she was pregnant and had made the mother of all mistakes—pardon the pun. But that didn't mean she was like her mother. She took care of herself, all by herself. And that's the way she liked it.

"We were together a long time ago," Kate said. "And a lot has changed since then."

"Yeah." Shadows slid through his eyes as he nodded. "You had my baby."

"And I wouldn't trade him for anything," she said fiercely. "I love that child more than I ever imagined it was possible to love anyone. Everything I do, every decision I make is for him."

"Okay. But I'm back now. If I'd been here…"

What would have been different? He'd dumped her. So what if it had taken her a while to let him know he was going to be a father? The decision was huge. Her own father had skipped out before she was old enough to remember him and Kate had often wondered why he'd bothered to marry her mom in the first place if he didn't plan to stick around. Joe had just done the not-sticking-around part up front.

Finally she said, "It's okay, Joe. It's not your fault you couldn't be here for J.T."

"But I'm here now."

"Yeah." And they needed to talk about what that meant. Real soon. But she wasn't ready yet.

"I want to do the right thing, Kate."

"What does that mean?"

More importantly, did she really want to hear this?

The uneasy feeling grew in her chest until she had trouble drawing in air. J.T. was hers. She could take care of him, support him, raise him to be a good man. She didn't want or need anyone's help for J.T. to be healthy and happy. If she didn't let anyone else in, the chances of keeping him happy went up. If she did it herself, she would know it was done right because she would always be there for him.

She looked at Joe and braced herself. "Define *the right thing*."

"We should get married."

Chapter Two

Kate was just taking a drink from her iced tea and nearly choked. "Don't you know it's not nice to make a joke when someone's drinking?"

Joe wasn't being funny. He was dead serious, although he hadn't intended to propose. If he'd planned it, there would have been flowers and candles, not harsh fluorescent lights. And the food would be better than flame-broiled cardboard with a shot of cholesterol. But now that the thought was out there, it felt right.

"I'm not joking. We should get married," he said.

"No, we shouldn't." She stabbed at the ice in her cup with the straw.

"Why not?"

"Do you really want me to start? The thing is, I only get a half hour for lunch," she said.

Irritation knotted inside him. He didn't remember her being this sarcastic. But then, all his memories were from before he'd told her they were over. She probably had reason to give him a hard time. Likely it'd be a good idea to let her get this out of her system.

"Take your best shot," he said. "Give me one good reason why it would be wrong."

"Just one?" she said, staring at him.

"For starters."

"Okay." She nodded thoughtfully. "Here's one. We hardly know each other."

"So marriage will give us a chance to get acquainted."

"Oh, please," she said. "That's just stupid."

"People do it all the time."

"Not this person." She twisted the dangling strands of her ponytail around her finger. "My life is all in place. Why would I want to turn it upside down?"

Speaking of upside-down life, he'd spent a whole lot of time in dark cellars, caves and God knows where else thinking about the baby. Her letter had said she was having a boy, right after she'd admitted she'd considered not telling him at all. That she was okay with raising the child alone and not to feel any obligation to be involved. *Be well and happy. Kate*, she'd signed the thing. He was well, but he hadn't been happy for longer than he could remember.

Scratch that. He'd been happy when he was with her. But more important than either of them was his son.

"What about the baby?" he asked.

"What about him?" she answered, her eyes flashing. "J.T. is perfect. I'm taking care of him just fine."

"In your letter you said you were okay with raising him alone, but—"

"I am," she interrupted. "Although I don't really remember what I said."

He remembered. He'd had it with him when he went down, hid the paper and read it so often he'd memorized every word while he'd been detained.

"You're looking pretty intense," she said warily.

"Just thinking." He leaned his forearms on the table. "Wouldn't you like some help with the baby?"

"I don't need help. Not from you."

"I'm J.T.'s father."

"That's a fact. And here's another one. You dumped me."

"I didn't know you were pregnant."

"Okay. But your gut instinct was to walk away from me. Now I'm supposed to believe that I'm the woman of your dreams because I had your baby?" She laughed, but there was no humor in it. "I don't think so."

"I was being deployed. It wasn't fair to ask you to wait."

"You didn't ask. You didn't give me a chance to decide if I wanted to wait for you. You just assumed and didn't give a rat's behind about how I felt. It was selfish."

Was that hurt in her eyes? He'd walked away because it was better for him, so he'd take responsibility for the selfish part. But he hadn't meant to hurt her. He'd been doing what was best for both of them.

If *best* was not being able to forget her, then his strategy had been a rousing success. If aching to feel her in his arms and see her bright smile and deep dimples was optimum, then his course of action had been a clear victory. If *best* was beating back the yearning to contact her, then he'd been right on.

The biggest hell of captivity, even worse than the beatings and losing another marine, was not being able to tell her he wanted his son. He wanted to be obligated, to be involved. To pick up where he'd walked out and start fresh. Who knows? They might have been married now. But judging by the resentment in her eyes and the edge to her voice, it was going to be an uphill battle.

"That time— Us— It's history," he said.

"And the past is where it's going to stay. Because the thing about you being selfish is that now I know. There's no taking it back. And it's a red flag for me that you're probably not very good marriage material."

"Now who's assuming?"

"It's not an assumption if you've got history to back it up."

He ran his fingers through his hair. It was longer than military issue now and felt weird, different. Kind of like this conversation. He'd dug himself a foxhole and now he had to fight his way out of it.

"The most important thing is J.T."

She nodded. "I agree."

"He needs a mother and a father."

"And he's got one of each. There's no reason to get wild and do something stupid."

"I want to be there for him," Joe said.

He'd nearly gone crazy, bound and blindfolded somewhere in the bowels of Afghanistan, knowing he was not only MIA as far as the military was concerned, but also during Kate's pregnancy and the birth of his child. Not knowing if Kate and the baby were okay. He couldn't be involved then because fate got in his way. But now he'd go to the mat with fate for the chance to know his son.

Kate frowned as she studied him. "Do you really believe a piece of paper and a couple of half-hearted 'I dos' are going to convince me that you're a forever-after kind of guy?"

Of course not. He had up-close-and-in-your-face experience that a marriage license didn't guarantee fidelity, loyalty and honesty. His ex-wife had barely waited until he'd deployed on his first tour before taking up with his brother. Out of sight, out of mind. But the betrayal was a double whammy and it had hurt so damn much that he didn't want to be in that situation again. He wouldn't let himself care. And he'd started to care too much for Kate so he'd broken it off.

The only good thing fate had done was deliver that letter before his last mission. Thoughts of seeing his son had gotten him through the darkest time of his life. He was here and Kate was going to have to deal with him.

"When it comes to J.T. I'm a forever-after kind of guy," he said.

"But you also brought up marriage and I keep coming back to the fact that I don't know you. Not then and not now." She pulled at the paper that had covered her straw, shredding it over the burger she'd barely touched. "On top of that, you're not the same man I knew before."

No kidding. He was a hard man. War had a way of doing that to you. Scenes flashed through his mind. The rat-a-tat of machine-gun fire. The whine of a mortar. The explosion of IEDs—improvised explosive devices—while he was inserting or extracting combat teams. Screams from the wounded. The knot in his belly when he landed in a hot zone and the wounded were hastily loaded on board. Taking off and flying his heart out to get them medical attention before it was too late.

The blood. The moans.

If a man didn't get hard, he didn't get through. You turned off the feelings to get the job done.

"And you're not the same woman I left behind. You can't go through the process of bringing a life into the world without it changing you."

"We finally agree about something. I *am* a mother now. I love J.T. more than anything in the world. And I'd do anything—" her eyes glowed with intensity "—*anything* in the world to protect him. It's my job."

"Is part of your job to protect him from his father?"

"It is if you're going to waltz in, make him love you then disappear."

Before he could respond to that, his pager went off. He pulled it out of his pocket and checked the digital display "Dispatch," he said. "The emergency code." He called and listened to whoever was on the other end at the office, then met her gaze. "I have to go. Another patient for Mercy Medical."

"I have to go back to work, too."

They both stood and he looked down at her. "This discussion isn't over, Kate."

She sighed. "I know."

Without another word, she walked away.

After picking J.T. up from Marilyn Watson, his babysitter, Kate took him home and changed quickly into shorts and a T-shirt. The baby fussed a little in his infant seat while she brushed her hair then put on a little blush and mascara. Earlier today, Joe had said they weren't finished talking. And judging by the look on his face, their conversation would continue soon. He'd surprised her last night, but this time she intended to be prepared for battle. He was a warrior, she intended to fight like a girl.

In the living room, she lifted her son from the infant seat, kissing his soft cheek. "It's bath time, Joey T."

Talking nonstop nonsense to him, she walked into the spare bath off the hall. After assembling soap and washcloth, and filling the J.T.-sized tub, she got the baby naked and sat him in the lukewarm water, one hand firmly holding his chubby upper arm. Squealing with delight, he splashed away. They both loved this nightly ritual because they were both tired after a long day. Evenings were rarely serene and she counted on this happy time before the unrestful portion of the program commenced.

"I saw your Dad—Daddy—" Kate stared at the baby who had just discovered his navel and was poking at it with one finger.

When Joe had ignored her letter telling him he was going to be a father, *daddy* was the last thing she would have called him. *Jerk* was on her list and a few other, even less flattering, names. Then she'd tried her darnedest to forget him.

Now she knew why he hadn't responded and her heart ached for him, what he must have gone through. She felt awful for believing the worst of him and knew part of that was about her own baggage before meeting him. But his rejection gave her more emotional baggage for the future.

Now he was back and they shared a child. There was every indication that he was dead serious about *sharing* this child.

She took the washcloth and washed her son's head, gently letting the water trickle over his face. "I got a marriage proposal today, J.T."

He blinked away moisture, then stared up at her with Joe's blue eyes. She'd always known he favored his father, but seeing the man again confirmed that as much as she'd wanted to forget Joe, she would always see him in their son. And something else hadn't changed.

In spite of the hurt and anger, Joe Morgan still made her knees weak and her heart beat too fast. That did not make her happy.

"Your daddy asked me to marry him." She decided *daddy* was okay. "What do you think about that?"

The baby grinned up at her, then hit the water with his free hand, sending it splashing everywhere. When Kate laughed, he gurgled out a giggle, wet, sloppy and joyous. She'd never known it was possible to love this much and every day her feelings for this little boy got bigger. She'd meant every word she'd said to Joe about protecting her child.

"So you like the idea of him being around, huh?"

J.T. splashed his approval, but Kate wasn't happy. Already he'd brought up the *M* word, but it had everything to do with the baby, not her. Nothing about J.T. was wrong, but tying herself legally to Joe because of that seemed like a disaster in the making.

Unlike her father, Joe had come back. But for how long? He'd given her the best four weeks of her life, then abruptly told her it was over. Why should she believe he wouldn't do that again? This time to J.T.?

She washed the baby all over and held on tight to her squirmy, slippery little guy. When he was rinsed, she lifted him out and wrapped a towel around him, although she was the wetter of the two. In his bedroom, she settled him on the changing table and handed him a toy to distract him while she put him in a diaper and lightweight jammies.

She brushed his dark hair with a baby brush and smiled tenderly down. "Life was a lot simpler yesterday, buddy. I only had to worry about you and me. When your daddy showed up, things got really complicated for Mommy."

Yesterday her life had been all about the stress of work and raising her son. Now she had conflict.

Kate carried him back to the living room and spread a big quilt on the floor, scattered some toys and put him down, hoping she'd have a few minutes to grab a frozen dinner before he demanded her attention. After popping one in the microwave, she turned the machine on.

J.T. didn't demand her attention, but the ringing doorbell got it in a big way. She didn't have to be psychic to know who was there. Looking down, she sighed at her wet front. She told herself the only reason she cared about her appearance was to make him regret walking away from her and the gullible part of her almost believed that.

The doorbell rang again and she looked through the peephole to confirm her suspicion. Then she said to J.T., "Someone's here to see you, big guy."

After turning the dead bolt, she opened the door and felt her heart race at the sight of all that tall, dark and handsome intensity. "Hi, Joe."

"Hi."

"Come in."

When he walked past, she inhaled the wonderful masculine scent. And speaking of masculine, he had a serious scattering of beard that had been five o'clock shadow several hours ago. Maybe he'd been in too big a hurry to shave. Or he knew how susceptible she was to the scruffy look.

She shut the door and found him staring down at the baby. The awed expression on his face worked over her hormones just as efficiently as the scruffy look.

"He's awake tonight," Joe said.

"And clean." The microwave beeped, signaling her dinner was done.

At the same time J.T. started to cry. Hurrying over, she scooped him up, then went into the kitchen and started to take the one-dish meal out of the oven.

"Can I hold him?" Joe asked.

She hesitated, something she would have done if a stranger on the street had asked her the same question. When his eyes narrowed, she knew Joe had noticed.

He wasn't a stranger. Not entirely. More important, he was J.T.'s father. "Sure."

When she put the child in his arms, Joe's intensity disappeared, replaced by tenderness. "Hey, buddy."

Kate watched her son as he stared up at his father with wide, wary eyes. He was a sturdy little guy and she didn't have to warn Joe about supporting his head. He'd missed that stage—not because he'd wanted to.

Joe met her gaze, something close to fatherly pride in his own. "He's pretty beefy."

"Yeah. He's always been a good eater."

"Has he?"

A twinge of regret fluttered through her because he'd missed that, too. And there was no way to make up for it. But this was a photo op if she'd ever seen one because he was holding his son for the first time.

"I have pictures," she said. "From the beginning."

"I'd like to see them." When he shifted the baby's weight in his arms, J.T.'s soft cheek brushed against the scruff of beard. The already skittish child let out a piercing wail. "Hey, pal, what's up?"

Looking awkward, Joe tried bouncing him, but this was unfamiliar territory and his body language said so, loud and clear. He was stiff, uncomfortable, and J.T. could feel it. His cries became more urgent—from zero to sobbing in three-point-two seconds.

Unfortunately, it was past his bedtime. J.T. was tired and beyond hope of being distracted.

"Let me have him," she said, taking the baby.

He wanted the comfort of nursing, another nightly ritual. Another something Joe hadn't seen and she wasn't comfortable doing it now. But as the baby got more and more upset and nuzzled his face into her shoulder, Kate knew there was no choice.

"What can I do?" he asked.

"He wants to nurse," she explained.

She went into the bedroom and grabbed a receiving blanket then sat on the couch hoping Joe would be as embarrassed as she was. Please God, he would take the hint and go.

When he stood his ground, she tugged up her shirt with as much dignity as possible, settled J.T. at her breast where he instantly latched on, then threw the blanket over her front. It was quiet now, except for the hum of the refrigerator.

"What happens during the day when you're at work?" Joe asked. "How does he— I mean, obviously you don't let him go hungry."

The man flew helicopters, complex machinery that was beyond the average person, but the basics of breast-feeding were a mystery. It might have made her smile if she weren't so tense about this complex mess they were in.

"I pump," she said.

"Iron? Gas? What?" he asked.

The puzzled expression on his face was so darn cute it made her even more tense and J.T. whimpered. "It's okay, sweet pea," she comforted. The sound of her voice quieted him and she felt him relax.

She looked up at Joe. He stood straight and tall with booted feet braced wide apart as if he were standing guard over them, which was oddly comforting. His worn jeans and snug black T-shirt molded to his body and left none of his muscles to her imagination. And she'd imagined him a lot since he walked out on her.

"I have a breast pump that extracts the milk," she explained. "It goes into bottles that I freeze and take to Marilyn Watson. She's the lady I told you about who watches him while I'm at work."

"I see."

"He's also starting solid food—cereal, fruit." She saw the look on his face and added, "Pureed fruit. No teeth yet."

"I got that." He almost smiled before the serious expression returned. "How did you learn all this stuff?"

"OJT—on-the-job training."

But she remembered when J.T. was brand-new and she'd felt

as if someone with a warped sense of humor had thrown her into the deep end of the parenting pool. She'd been alone. On her own with a newborn. Trying to breast-feed, not knowing if J.T. was getting enough to eat. That first night the two of them cried together. But she got through it by herself. That's how it always had been and always would be.

By the heavy, relaxed feel of him, she knew J.T. had fallen asleep. She stood and said, "I'm going to put him to bed."

Joe nodded, but to her relief didn't follow her into the other room. She placed the baby on his back with a light receiving blanket over his legs. It was May in Las Vegas and far from cold. The gesture was more of a "mom thing" than a necessity to keep him warm. After adjusting her shirt more modestly, she rejoined Joe.

"I got your dinner ready," he said.

He'd set it on the bar with a glass of iced tea beside it. Although she wasn't hungry now, she knew she needed to eat something and sat down. He stood in the kitchen across from her.

"Thanks."

He shrugged. "I know how to get food in and out of a microwave."

The subtext of that remark was that he didn't know what to do with a baby. The pained regret in his expression made her want to comfort him. "Having a child might be the most natural thing in the world, but they don't come with an instruction manual."

"I'm sorry I wasn't here."

She took a bite of mystery meat and studied him while she chewed and swallowed. All she could think to say was, "It's not your fault, Joe."

And it wasn't. But when she'd received no response from him, she hadn't known he was a prisoner in Afghanistan and the silence had hurt her deeply. For the second time. She never wanted to hurt like that again.

"I'll never know what it was like to hold him as a newborn."

"If it's any consolation, he won't remember that." She finished off the mashed potatoes and washed them down with iced tea. "And it's a good thing. I was all thumbs and he was so tiny. It took time to know what I was doing."

"That's all I'm asking for, Kate." He rested muscular forearms on the countertop in front of her. His eyes sparked with intensity as they met hers. "All I want is time to know my son and learn how to take care of him. Time for him to know me, to trust me."

"That's the hard part," she said. "Why should I believe you'll stick around?"

Why should she believe he was different from the other men she'd known? The ones who'd paraded in and out of her mother's life when she was a child. Each time she'd hoped and prayed this one would stay so she could have a family—a mom and dad like other kids. It had never happened and she didn't want J.T. to know the same disappointment she had.

Joe looked down for several moments, then met her gaze. "I guess there's nothing I can say to convince you. But, here's the thing. I wasn't here when you were pregnant or for the first months of his life. I *will* be around now. Count on it."

She had to be fair; there was no choice but to give him time with his child. He was entitled to that. It wasn't his problem that her attraction for him refused to die. Since there was no way she'd let J.T. out of her sight, she'd have to see him—and do her best to make sure history didn't repeat itself.

The last time he'd only wanted sex. Now he was there for the baby. It had nothing to do with her, and she needed to remember that. She'd already experienced a serious level of pain on Joe's account that was a small preview of the damage he could do to her heart.

"Okay," she said. "You can come over." Then she held up her finger in warning. "Just don't bring up marriage again."

As if that would protect her from emotional catastrophe. She could only hope.

Chapter Three

Kate had said okay—permission to come aboard as a parent. It was bright and early the following morning and he stood on her doorstep with bagels and doughnuts in hand. He didn't bring coffee because after browsing breast-feeding sites on the Net, he wasn't sure whether J.T. would get caffeine through his mom. On general principle he figured it wasn't good for a baby.

Joe knocked softly on the door in case the baby might still be asleep. He didn't know a lot about this, but the little information he had suggested new parents were tired, which meant babies didn't sleep much.

Kate answered the door with a coffee cup in her hand which answered the caffeine question. "Hi. You're early."

And you're beautiful.

For a split second he was afraid he'd said that out loud. It was the honest-to-God truth, but she wouldn't want to hear it from him. Her sunstreaked brown hair was tousled from sleep and he remembered it looking like that after he'd run his hands through the silky strands all night long. She was wearing white shorts and a sleeveless green cotton shirt. Her feet were bare and her face didn't have even a trace of makeup. She took his breath away and also, apparently, his powers of speech because he hadn't said a word yet.

"Hi." He gave her the bag. "Breakfast."

"Thanks. Come in."

He followed her inside and said, "I wasn't sure about coffee and caffeine for J.T.—"

She held up her cup. "It's decaf and I miss my morning jolt. Want some?"

The sight of her had already given him a jolt and no caffeine was involved. "Coffee would be great." He looked around and saw J.T. propped up in a high chair and gnawing on something that looked like a bread stick. He had goo and residue, presumably from a food source of unknown origin in his hand, all over his face and as far down his body as was visible. He reached to the top of his head and ran a grubby hand in his hair, grabbing a hank before pulling it straight up.

"Hey, buddy." He walked over and squatted in front of the boy who was watching him with big, interested blue eyes. "You've got a punk-rock thing going on there."

"I wouldn't get too close," Kate warned, coffeepot in hand. "He's a mess."

"Yeah. I have visual confirmation," he said wryly.

"He's pretty quick with those hands if you're not careful. Just like you—" She stopped and her cheeks turned pink. "Never mind."

Impossible not to mind when she reminded him of how good the sex had been. Not that he needed much reminding. But she was right. It was better not to go there.

He smiled at the baby. "What's up, J.T.?"

"He is," Kate said, glancing over her shoulder. "And a lot during the night, too. I think he's teething. As a matter of fact, that gross thing in his hand is a teething biscuit. He likes to chew on it. Keeps him busy for a long time."

Joe moved to the bar and watched her put sugar and fat-free half and half in her steaming mug. She was very particular about it, he remembered now. Coffee was practically a religious experience.

With another cup in her hand, she moved to the counter, keeping the bar between them. "Here you go."

"Thanks." He took the steaming mug from her and set it down to cool. Black was how he liked it.

There was nothing like the smell of a good cup of coffee. Unless it was the sweet scent of Kate. The fragrance of her skin drifted to him and all he could think about was fresh flowers and feminine heat. For a woman who hadn't had a good night's sleep, she looked awfully darn appealing. For a man who'd given her up, he was still pretty damn attracted. What had he been thinking?

That was a no-brainer. He'd walked before she could. He didn't want to get burned again. It was as simple as that. But there was nothing simple about the way he got lost in her big, expressive eyes.

"You're here for a crash course in child care. So—" She dragged out the single word, then took a sip of coffee. Nervous. Good. It wasn't just him.

"Not quite the way I'd phrase it," he said and couldn't help smiling. "More like the basics of baby boot camp."

"Well put."

"Where do we start?"

She glanced over her shoulder at the gurgling; babbling baby. "Bath first. Do you want to get him out of the chair?"

He blew out a breath. "A pilot has to take the controls sooner or later."

"Just remember he's really sturdy and crying is actually good for his lungs."

But not so good for my heart, Joe thought.

Last night, his son had cried because he didn't know his own father. Joe had felt angry, powerless to help, and it had made him hurt in a place he'd never known existed. He hated that. Kate had easily handled the situation. But she had a four-month headstart. More than that if you counted the time she'd carried the boy inside her. It was the time Joe could never get back which had sparked his anger. All he could do was start now and learn, because he never wanted to feel that helpless again.

He started to lift the child out of the chair, then released the seat belt when he got hung up. The baby's feet caught on the tray and, with one arm around J.T.'s waist, he untangled them.

"And we have lift off." In more ways than one, he thought when there was an unmistakable sound from the region of the baby's tush. Sniffing, he said, "Tell me that isn't what I think."

Kate grinned and it could only be described as evil, with a little wicked thrown in for good measure. "There's never been a better time for diaper-changing 101."

Joe groaned. He held the boy in both hands, out in front of him so as not to squish anything any more than necessary.

Kate instructed him to put the baby down on the changing table, which was the easy part. Keeping him there was like trying to lasso a hurricane. His son wanted to roll sideways, chew on his feet and grab tubes, tissues and everything else lined up for this operation. Joe felt a trickle of sweat on his back, not unlike the first time he'd taken the controls of a helicopter.

"You're going to need wet wipes and lots of them," Kate said, amusement dripping from every word.

With one hand firmly on the baby's midsection, he looked at her. "You're enjoying this way too much."

"I know." She smiled.

"You're not even going to deny it?"

"Nope." She shook her head. "This is just too good for words."

She verbally walked him through the process, but remained hands-off while he struggled to keep small hands and feet out of the radioactive zone. Then she told him what he could do with it, the diaper that is. Who knew there was a gizmo that magically contained odors? There was a good reason it was called a Diaper Genie.

"Mission accomplished."

"Not so fast, Marine." She laughed. "You're not finished yet. It's bath time."

Lord have mercy, he thought. Words that struck terror into his warrior soul. At least she took pity on him and put out the supplies, then filled the tiny tub. Keeping the baby contained in it was diaper-changing bad times ten. Holding on to a slippery baby was like trying to steady his chopper in a twister. When goo and God knows what else was washed off, Kate handed him the towel. Probably not because she wanted to help him as much as because she didn't want the baby to get cold.

"I've put out his clothes," she explained.

"Changing table?" He held back the groan.

"You're catching on."

Not really, but he was glad she thought so. When he put J.T. down, Kate handed the baby a toy that went straight in his mouth. It also kept his hands busy. She could have done that before.

"Here's a fresh diaper." She held out a small, folded, not-quite-square white thing.

"Where are the schematics and operating manual?"

She laughed and opened the square, sliding it under the baby's bottom, getting in close to Joe's side. Her shoulder brushed his arm and he swore there were sparks. She glanced at him, then stepped sideways.

"Just cover him and hook the tabs," she instructed. "Here's a onesy."

"A what?"

"It's a shirt that snaps between his legs so it won't ride up. One piece. A onesy."

"Not a very manly name."

"Trust me. You're the only one offended. J.T. is all about being comfortable."

At least one of them was. With her so close, Joe was anything but comfortable. Not to mention soaked. He was as soaked as she'd been the night before, but it looked much better on her. The wet shirt she'd been wearing had been practically transparent. Molded to her full breasts it had made her look like a randy teenage boy's best dream.

He hadn't known at that point, but it had been only the first temptation of the evening. If there was any silver lining to J.T.'s meltdown, it had been the glimpse of her creamy skin when she'd fed his son from her body. The message had come through loud and clear that she wanted him to leave. But he'd already missed too much to retreat at the signs of hostility in her eyes. And he was glad he'd stood his ground. It had been the most beautiful sight he'd ever seen.

A high-pitched squeal pulled him back to the present. J.T. was rubbing a chubby fist in his eye, following the action with a big yawn. It didn't take a rocket scientist to know he was tired. That made two of them. Babies were definitely high-maintenance.

"Nap time?" he asked, looking at Kate.

She nodded and he felt as if he'd deciphered intel that would bring down a whole terrorist network. "But he has to eat something first."

"Again? The teething biscuit wasn't enough?" He picked the boy up. The feel of the baby weight in his arms was a little better. "Scratch that. He was wearing most of it."

"You're very observant."

He watched Kate prepare a baby bottle she took from the freezer, which was probably the pumped breast milk she'd told him about. When it was ready, she settled him on the couch with J.T. in his arms.

"I think you can figure it out from here," she said, hovering close by.

He put the bottle up to the small mouth and the kid latched on. At least one of them knew what to do. And that's when it hit him that he was feeding his child for the first time. This was a photo moment of monumental proportions. This was huge.

The baby must have felt some of these vibes because he started squirming.

"It's okay, buddy. Easy does it," he said softly.

That seemed to calm him because he started sucking again. After draining the bottle, he let out a big burp.

He grinned at Kate. "I'm so proud."

"You're such a guy," she said, rolling her eyes.

When J.T. heaved a satisfied sigh, Joe wondered what to do now. Then the baby closed his eyes and the sight made Joe's chest grow tight. A second later something expanded and moved through him, filling up some of the empty places in his soul.

He'd done Marine Corps boot camp, flown helicopters in Afghanistan until his eyes felt as though all the desert sand was in them. But he'd never felt as tired as he did now. Being a father

was hard work—in the most awesome possible way. What if
he had *never* received the letter?

Thinking about the fact that Kate was pregnant with his son
had kept him going in his darkest hours. And suddenly he
wondered how she'd found out where to send the letter.

"Do you want me to put him in his crib?" she asked.

"No. I like holding him." Understatement of the century.
"Can I ask you something?"

She sat on the couch beside him. "Sure."

"When I was deployed overseas—" He met her gaze. "—how
did you get my address?"

"From your brother."

Preston Morgan. The man who'd betrayed him and broken
up his marriage. That was freaking perfect. Unfortunately their
dad's death had left them partners in Southwestern Helicopters.
Because of that his attorney brother needed to know how to
reach him. It should have been obvious that Kate had gone to
him for the information. He just hadn't wanted to think about
what that meant.

"What's wrong?" Kate asked, frowning at him.

The easy answer was that he didn't want his bastard of a
brother anywhere near Kate. The hard question was why it
mattered so much that the thought of it enraged him.

"It's not important."

"No? Then why do you look like that?"

"Like what?"

"Like you want to choke someone. I know your brother is
here in Las Vegas so I went to see him. He was extremely kind
and very helpful."

That wasn't a big surprise. Kate was an incredibly beautiful woman, not unlike his ex-wife. Preston had hit on her
without regard for legal or family ties. The thought of Kate in

a compromising situation like that tightened the knot in his gut. "I'll just bet he was ready to lend a hand."

She didn't look happy. "He said if I needed anything while you were gone to call. And to be sure and let him know when he was an uncle."

"Did you?"

"No." Her full lips pulled into a straight line for a moment. "When I didn't hear from you, I thought it best not to."

Well, thank goodness for that. The thought of his brother anywhere near her bent his rotors big time. "Smart move."

"Obviously you disapprove of what I did." Her eyes narrowed. "It would be helpful to have more information, Joe. I don't know what's going on between you—"

"Nothing." Not any more. Not ever again. He'd looked up to his big brother once, wanted to be like him. Their father had thought Preston was perfect and Joe was the screwup. Not so much.

"Where else was I supposed to go? Would it be better if I hadn't written to you at all?"

"No." The word was sharp and his voice louder than he'd intended.

J.T. began to squirm and whimper as his tiny fists started waving. Then he let out a wail. Joe wasn't sure what he'd done, but it wasn't good.

Kate stood and held out her arms. "I'll take him."

He let her because she knew what to do and he didn't want to make things worse. She walked down the hall, murmuring soothing sweet nothings and the silence proved it had worked.

Joe restlessly paced the living room because he was angry as hell. At Kate, but mostly at himself. He'd thought the past no longer affected him. He was wrong. And being wrong had affected his son.

It was obvious that Kate was confused and wanted to know what was up between him and his brother, but talking about it was the last thing he wanted. About that, and especially about what happened to him in Afghanistan. As long as there was breath left in his body, he would move heaven and earth not to let any of his darkness upset his son again. And Kate. He couldn't stand the thought of anything bad touching her.

Kate wondered about Joe's sudden shift in mood. One minute he was gentle and soft, the next tense, angry, and the baby had felt something—his aggression, hostility. That definitely defined the man after she'd said his brother had given her the address. What was up with that?

While the baby slept, she and Joe sat at the kitchen table munching on doughnuts and bagels and drinking the coffee that had gone cold. She'd nuked it.

Needing something to take the edge off what felt far too intimate, she had a pencil and paper and was jotting down things to get at the store. Every time she looked up, he was watching her.

"What?" she asked.

He nodded at her growing list. "You're going to need a U-Haul."

"Sometimes it feels that way. Especially when I'm toting J.T. along. I don't think I truly appreciated shopping by myself until becoming a mother."

"I could help."

"I wasn't complaining," she said quickly.

"That never occurred to me. After going through basic training this morning, I have a better understanding. Shopping with the little guy must be similar to the precision and coordination of inserting a combat team into a hot zone."

She laughed. "Sometimes it feels that way."

"So let me help. I could go for you."

"Thanks, but no. I've seen men in the store. Without a cell phone they're lost. It would take twice as long."

"Then I could stay with J.T.—"

"No." When his eyes narrowed, she wanted to call the word back. Or at least soften her tone. "What if he wakes up?"

"I'll handle it. Crying is actually good for his lungs, remember?"

And how she wanted *those* words back. "I'm more worried about you."

"I wouldn't hurt him."

"That's not what I meant." Not really. But his sudden change of mood before had taken her aback. "The crying can frazzle you even if you're used to it."

"I'm pretty tough—"

The phone rang and she was grateful for the interruption until the caller ID showed that it was her mother. Nonetheless, dealing with Candy Carpenter was easier than explaining to Joe why she didn't want to leave him alone with his son.

She picked up the phone and hit the talk button. "Hi, Mom."

"Hi. How's J.T.?"

"Really good."

"And you?"

"I'm fine." A lie, but she wasn't saying anything about her baby's father showing up while he was sitting there watching her. "How are things with you?"

"Robert and I had a fight."

So this wasn't a call to see how things were with her and J.T. It was all about her mother. She glanced at Joe who was watching her. "I'm sorry to hear that."

A big sigh came through loud and clear. "He said I wasn't

giving him enough space. That I was going too fast and he's not ready."

"Were you?"

"No."

Kate rolled her eyes. Her mother lived in Pahrump, about an hour's drive northwest of Las Vegas. She worked as a waitress in a diner. An attractive brunette, she got a lot of male attention. All was well in the first stages of a new relationship— first-meet euphoria followed by a few weeks of adoration. And of course, Candy always swore this one was the love of her life and they'd be together forever. Then she started to push.

Kate had told her over and over that she didn't need a man to be happy, but somehow the words never stuck. She was tired of wasting her breath.

"Did it ever occur to you that you might be better off?" she asked.

"How can you say that?" Candy demanded. "He's every-thing I ever wanted. Good-looking. He has a great job. We have fun together. The sex is—"

"Too much info, Mom." That wasn't a visual she wanted in her head.

"I'm still a young and vibrant woman."

"Yes, you are. And you're okay on your own. There's no point in hanging on to something that doesn't make your life better."

"He does make it better," Candy protested.

"That's not what I'm hearing."

"If he'd just give us time we could work it out."

"That's the thing, Mom. You're trying to speed things up instead of giving it time."

"You don't understand."

No, she didn't. "Look, Mom, J.T. is starting to fuss. I have to go," she lied.

"Give him a kiss from me."

"Will do. Bye." She replaced the phone and looked at Joe.

"Problem?" he asked.

"Just the usual."

"Define *usual*."

Apparently she'd never told him about her mother. But then, they'd been so wrapped up in each other talking hadn't been high on their list of activities.

"The usual is the latest in an inappropriate string of men she's gotten too possessive with. My father being one."

"Oh?"

There was no reason she could come up with off the top of her head not to tell him. "My mother was pregnant when she married my father. What I don't get is why he bothered when he didn't plan to stick around. I never met the man."

Joe's eyes turned dark, a sign he didn't approve, except that this time it wasn't about her. "Maybe you're better off."

"That thought has crossed my mind." In fact, she'd just said it to her mom about the current flavor of the month. "But over the years she's had a string of men. My father was just the first mistake."

"Is that why you refused my marriage proposal?"

"Partly."

Again she could see no reason not to admit the truth. Sometimes she'd liked a man her mother brought home, but found out caring was a mistake because they always left. There was one she'd disliked on sight, and she'd begged her mom to dump him, gave her an ultimatum—him or me. Candy had chosen him. So Kate had left home and made a rule: she would rely only on herself and not make a mistake that would ruin her life. Now J.T. was her life and not making a mistake was more important than ever.

"What's the other part?" he asked.

She met his gaze. "My biggest fear is turning into my mother. Always looking for a man. Always hoping he'll be the one to take care of me. I don't need anyone."

"So no man gets in?"

"That's right."

That was a lie. He'd gotten in, Dashing, daring Marine Corps helicopter pilot Joe Morgan. His good looks and confident, compelling charm had taken her prisoner with no shots fired. The probing intensity of his eyes and his devil-may-care attitude had made her feel alive. She'd been sleepwalking through life until she'd met him and then she'd decided she would be a fool not to enjoy every moment he wanted to spend with her. She'd never lived a great story and that's all he was ever supposed to be, until he became so much more.

Then, without warning, he said they were over and she'd been blindsided and desperately hurt. As long as he was playing father and insisted on being in her face, she was vulnerable to all the emotional harm he could do her. But she was probably borrowing trouble. How long could Joe's fatherly devotion last? Based on the collective experience of the Carpenter women, men didn't stick around. Kate hoped that would be the case with Joe.

He was the only man who'd ever made her break her rule and it had gone badly. He'd left her heart in pieces and she didn't want to give him another shot at destroying what was left.

Chapter Four

While he had one hand on J.T.'s belly to hold him in place on the changing table, Joe used the other to fold up the dirty disposable diaper and stuff it into the container. He pulled a clean one from the stack on the shelf, applied powder, got the gizmo on right side up and pressed the tabs in place.

"Mission accomplished." He grinned at the baby, who smiled and squealed and kicked his legs.

Had it only been a week since he'd fed his son for the first time? Seven days that had forever altered his center of gravity. This child was the most important thing.

Joe had changed shifts with one of the other chopper pilots so his days off coincided with Kate's. Fortunately it had worked to the other guy's advantage because Joe hadn't wanted to pull rank. It was his helicopter company, but being the boss from hell didn't inspire loyalty. The change had worked out pretty well. He and his brother never saw each other and the company was more successful than his father had ever imagined.

He wondered if his dad would be proud of him. Now that he was a father, Joe wondered about a lot of things. And he was learning a lot about the importance of routine in child-rearing. It seemed mornings were the best. J.T. was happy and so was Kate. After breakfast, the baby played, and when he got crabby it was time for a nap. Then it was lunchtime and a trip to a nearby park, weather permitting. Pretty soon it would be too hot. By that time Joe figured he could take the baby to his place in Spanish Trails. The pool would cool them off. He'd teach J.T. how to swim. There were so many things he wanted to teach him. Baseball. Cars. Girls.

About girls… Every time Joe thought of Kate a wave of lust shot through him—primitive and powerful. Not just because she was beautiful. She had a tender way with the baby that blew him away. And when he looked at her mouth… All he could think about was kissing her to see if she still tasted as sweet and sexy as he remembered.

But giving in to the temptation was counterproductive. They shared a child and he was struggling to find a foothold in fatherhood. It didn't take top secret intel to know that Kate wasn't overly keen on him being around. His reaction to the fact that she'd talked to his brother hadn't helped.

He'd seen her surprise, the questions and doubts. The thing was, it had surprised him, too. He didn't care about his wife cheating on him with his brother. Not any more. But something about Kate in the same room with Preston Morgan had made his blood boil. And he knew she was watching him. One false move and he was out of there. Or at least she'd try to get him out.

He snapped the onesy and pulled on the tiny denim shorts. "Your old man is getting the hang of this, pal."

In response, J.T. waved his arms, and when his hands accidentally bumped, he became totally absorbed in his fingers. As if he'd never seen them before.

"Come on. Let's go see your mom."

Joe lifted the boy into his arms and walked back to the living room where Kate was folding clothes.

"Hi, big boy," she said smiling.

"I'm going to assume you mean J.T.," he teased.

"What was your first clue?"

"The tone." Not once in the time they'd spent together had she called him big boy and if she had, there would have been a sultry, sexy sound wrapped around the syllables.

The pink in her cheeks told him her thoughts were following a similar track. "He looks happy now," she said, changing the subject.

That was okay with him. It was stupid to think about the past, let alone bring it up. Neither of them wanted to go there. But every time he saw her, there was no stopping the visions of tangled legs and twisted sheets. His brain circuits overheated and the comments he kept in a mental holding pattern flew out of his mouth.

Joe set the baby on the blanket in the middle of the floor and handed him a rattle, which he grabbed and stuck in his mouth. Talking about their son was safe territory. He sat down beside him, at Kate's feet. She reached into the laundry basket and pulled out a small garment.

"How did it feel to be pregnant?" he asked.

"Wow. Where do I start?" Her hands dropped into her lap as a faraway look came into her eyes. "When I did the home pregnancy test, the first thing I felt was fear at that plus sign. I just couldn't believe it."

"After that? When you got used to the idea, what went through your mind?"

"I had to make plans. And see a doctor. Not necessarily in that order." She met his gaze. "It was scary. But—"

"What?" he urged, seeing the soft expression on her face.

"When I felt him move the first time—" She stopped, searching for words. "I thought it was gas. Sort of like bubbles. Fluttering. Then the movements got stronger. And the miracle of it all began to sink in. I had the privilege of carrying a new life inside me. I won't lie to you—it was awesome."

He smiled, even as the emptiness of being left out drifted through him. "I'm sorry I missed it."

"I could have done without looking like a beached whale and ankles so full of water they could float a battleship, and labor wasn't fun. But when the nurse put him in my arms for the first time—" She sighed. "It was worth everything."

He'd *give* everything to have seen her grow big with his child. It wasn't about avoiding the bad stuff he'd gone through in Afghanistan. It was about being deprived of the good stuff he could never get back.

Again he said, "I'm sorry I missed it. I would have—"

"I know," she said. "It's okay."

"No, it's not." He watched J.T. roll from his back to his stomach, then stretch out chubby fingers for a bright-yellow rubber duck. When Joe squeezed the whistling sound out of it, the baby stilled, studied, then grabbed it and lowered his mouth to chew on it. "But I got here as quick as I could."

"I know you did." She met his gaze and her own was gentle with sympathy. "Looking back, it would have been nice not to be so alone." She caught his surprised look and quickly added, "My mom was there when he was born. But I mean when they put him in my arms the magnitude of the whole thing hit me. I was responsible for his life. He was dependent on me for his survival and I didn't know what I was doing."

"I don't know how much help I would have been."

She shrugged. "I handled it. Baptism of fire. Jumped into the water with both feet. There was no choice. And somehow I got through it—one day at a time."

"Yeah." He'd been doing the same thing. But instead of an innocent new life to show for it, he'd found only violence and death. And more black marks on his soul.

"I was serious when I said it's on-the-job training. Now it's offered on a continually exhausting basis."

"You'll get no argument from me." He rested his hand on his son's back and the rise and fall of his small chest, the warmth of his little body, chased away some of the darkness.

"There are up sides to all the work."

"Satisfaction of a job well done?" he asked.

She nodded. "That. And it keeps me in shape."

There wasn't a damn thing wrong with her shape. His gaze lowered to her curvy legs in shorts that were long enough to be modest, but brief enough to make him hold his breath as he waited for them to slide up and reveal more smooth, soft skin. He swallowed hard as he remembered those legs wrapped around his waist and her eyes glazed with passion.

"You're not alone now, Kate."

Their gazes locked and something similar simmered in her eyes, a look he remembered far too well. It's what had attracted him the first time he'd seen her. She'd been attracted to him, too, and couldn't quite hide it. Now the pulse in her neck fluttered like crazy, and when she folded the last of the laundry and set it on the pile, her hand trembled.

"I need to put this stuff away." She stood and lifted the stack then disappeared down the hall.

Beside him J.T. started jabbering, the nonsensical sounds

Kate had told him were the beginning of language. "I sure know how to clear a room, pal—"

A harsh beeping interrupted him and he knew it was her pager on the kitchen counter. She hurried back into the room and picked up the beeper to look at the digital display. "It's the hospital."

While she made a phone call, he played with the baby. He lifted him high over his head and the boy laughed, making him laugh, too—something he would have doubted was possible considering how tense he was. When he lowered his arms, J.T. grabbed his nose and giggled when he snorted.

He was half listening when Kate made another phone call to Marilyn the babysitter. She needed her to watch J.T. because she'd been called in to work.

She hung up and turned to look at him. "They're short a nurse in the E.R."

"Okay."

"I'm first call. That means—"

"If they're short-handed you have to go in."

"Right." She twisted her fingers together. "So I have to go."

"I got that."

"I'm taking J.T. to the babysitter."

"That's not necessary, Kate. I'm already here. I'm ready, willing and able to fly solo with him."

Something close to panic darkened her eyes. "I can't ask you to do that."

"So you'd rather leave him with the young grandmother who has references?" Anger knotted in his belly.

"Marilyn has watched him since my maternity leave ended and I had to go back to work. She loves him like her own grandson."

"But he's not hers. He's my flesh and blood. Not just a job I get paid for."

Joe tamped down the annoyance the same way he'd pushed aside fear when he flew a chopper into a hot zone, or planned his escape from a terrorist nightmare. Thoughts of seeing his son—and Kate—had gotten him through hell and back. He wasn't sure what he'd expected, but this wasn't it. He'd never anticipated that she wouldn't trust him.

What else was he supposed to think? If there was an Olympic event for excuses, Kate would take the gold. He was done pretending he didn't notice.

"Why won't you leave me alone with my son?" he said bluntly.

She walked over, took the baby from him, and cuddled him close. When she bent over to pick up a toy, Joe's gut tightened at the sight of her shapely backside and those short shorts showing off a whole lot of leg. The fact that he could even notice at a time like this made him either the world's biggest loser or jackass. Or both. That thought didn't sweeten his mood.

Then she stood in front of him, so close he could smell the floral scent of her skin and feel the heat of her body. She was all womanly curves and feminine fierceness.

With the light of battle in her eyes, she said, "We've been through this before, Joe. I don't really know you."

He held out his finger and J.T. grabbed it. "I love this boy."

"It's been a little over a week and you get points for showing up. But that's not very long."

"What we have here is a catch-22. I need time on the books to prove I'm in this for the long haul, but you won't give me the chance to put in the hours."

God, this was frustrating. How could he convince her he was sincere?

"I can't take a chance," she said, her voice quivering with emotion. "He's my baby and I won't let him get hurt."

"He's my baby and I won't hurt him." Joe took a step forward.

She took a step back. "I will not let you insinuate yourself into his life then break his heart when you don't stick around. It's an unacceptable risk."

"I'm not a risk. I'm a sure thing." All he could give her was his word. "I'm not your father, Kate. I'm not the kind of man who abandons his own kid."

She lifted her determined chin just a little higher. "That's not what this is about."

"On what planet?"

She'd told him that in her whole life no man had stayed. Including him. But that was about not wanting to ask her to wait while he deployed. It was about not wanting to trust and risk having the rug pulled out from under him.

The fact was, this was fallout because he'd walked away, and from her perspective, had never looked back. They both knew that wasn't his choice; still, he understood she felt burned because of a long history of getting burned.

He ran his fingers through his hair. "I'm not like the losers your mother hooks up with."

"I should never have told you that. That's not what this is about," she said.

"Yeah, it is."

"Whatever. It's not important. What matters is that I'm J.T.'s mother. I'm just trying to do what I think is best for him."

"I get that. And from your perspective of growing up without a father, wouldn't you say having two parents is the better way to go? Are you afraid for J.T.? Or yourself?"

She backed up another step, her eyes growing wide. "In the future, I'll have to be careful not to give you ammunition to use against me."

It was low even for him, but he wanted to see his son. There was a level of low he hadn't hit yet. "Consider this." He folded his arms over his chest. "If we can't do this the easy way, we'll do it the hard way. But we will do it."

"What are you talking about?" Her lips trembled and she caught the top one between her teeth and tightened her hold on the baby.

"I'm talking about getting a lawyer and petitioning for my rights. It's not a step I want to take."

"Why should I believe that?"

"Because it's hard to co-parent when the one with physical custody hates your guts. I don't want to create hard feelings, Kate. That's the truth. But if you keep putting up roadblocks, I will fight you."

The gauntlet was thrown and she needed to think about it so he kissed J.T. and left. At the bottom of the stairs, he paused as the hot Vegas sun beat down on him. He blew out a long breath and shook his head. That might not have been the best move he could have made.

For one thing, it might have tipped the scales toward her hating his guts anyway. And that wasn't the best way to get time with his son. And time in Kate's bed. There was no point in running from the honest truth. He still wanted her.

Hell, he'd never stopped wanting her.

Kate walked out of Trauma Room Three. Her patient was a young mother, Lucy Castillo, broadsided when another car ran a stop sign. She'd been medevaced to Mercy Medical by helicopter, but her child, in the accident with her, had been brought in by paramedics. The little girl was only six. Lucy had begged Kate to check on her child. She needed to know her baby was okay before she went to surgery.

It didn't take Kate long to find out. She checked at the nurses' station, then decided to see the little girl for herself. If she were in this situation, she'd want someone to give J.T. some personal attention. As she walked down the hall, a deep voice drifted to her. She'd heard that same voice just yesterday when he'd threatened a legal fight for visitation rights. And then he'd asked if she was afraid for herself.

The privacy curtain wasn't drawn and when she got to Trauma Room Ten, she recognized Joe. He was in his flight suit and sat beside the gurney, talking quietly to Patty Castillo who was alert and had just been shaken up in the accident. She backed away without being seen and returned to the worried mother to put her mind at rest. The little girl's father was on his way, but he was coming across the valley through rush-hour traffic.

Kate started to go to the cafeteria to grab a break while she could, but she couldn't forget the sight of Joe with that little girl in Trauma Room Ten. His job ended when the patient he'd airlifted to Mercy Medical was offloaded and brought in for treatment, yet there he sat with a frightened child he wasn't responsible for.

When she stopped outside the room again, she heard the little girl, then peeked inside.

"I want to see my mommy."

"You will, Patty. In a little while. I promise."

"When, Joe? It's been forever."

He was on a first-name basis with her. The Morgan charm worked fast. That shouldn't be a surprise. No one knew the power of it better than Kate.

"Right now the doctors are taking care of your mom."

"Why couldn't I go on your helicopter with her?"

Kate knew why. Lucy Castillo had abdominal injuries and was losing blood. The trauma team had a "golden hour," the time when swift intervention literally made the difference between life and death. Only one patient could fit in the chopper and for Patty's mom the quick flight meant life.

Joe held the child's little hand between his own. "I brought her here fast so the doctors could take care of her sooner."

"But I'm not hurt so bad, right?"

"Right. That's why you got to take a ride in the big truck."

Patty frowned at him. "There was lots of stuff in there. But the para—"

"Paramedics," Joe said helpfully.

"Yeah. Paramedics. One was a lady. She was nice."

"You're pretty easy to be nice to."

"If I'm not hurt bad, why did they hafta put the needle in my arm with the tube on it?"

"It's just a precaution— In case they needed to give you some medicine fast to make you better. But you're okay and they didn't have to do that."

"When is my daddy coming?" she asked.

"I'm not sure. Would you like me to go check for you?"

"Not yet." She clutched his sleeve. "In a little while."

"Okay. I'm not going anywhere."

As easy as that, Kate mused. You'd have thought being there for a frightened little girl was the only thing a highly skilled, incredibly successful businessman helicopter pilot had on his agenda at the moment.

"I'm scared, Joe. If you had to get Mommy here so fast, that means she was hurt really bad. What if she—"

He put a gentle finger on her mouth to shush the words. "Don't borrow trouble."

"'Cuz I hafta pay it back?"

"How do you know about paying back?" he asked, humor in his voice.

"When I wanted a toy at the store and Mommy said no, I

asked if I could buy it with my money. She said I didn't have money until I got my allowance. If I borrowed it early, I'd hafta pay it back."

"I see." He coughed to smother a chuckle. "It doesn't work the same way with trouble."

"We had trouble today," she said, sniffling. "I was so scared. Mommy screamed just before—" With a small fist, she rubbed tears from her eyes. "Does this mean I'm a crybaby?"

"No." He took her hand. "This time it's okay, Patty. I know how it feels to be scared."

"But you're a man."

"Men get scared sometimes."

"What scared you?" she asked, awe in her voice.

"Something happened to my helicopter when it was in the air and I knew it wouldn't stay up."

"An accident? Like me and Mommy?"

"Not exactly. But it was pretty scary. I got through it by thinking about someone I love."

"Who?" the little girl asked.

Before he could answer, a man brushed past Kate. He was tall, dark-haired and worried. When Joe looked up, he noticed her in the doorway, then stood and backed away from the gurney.

"Daddy!"

"Hi, baby." The frantic father bent and kissed his daughter's forehead.

"Where's Mommy?"

"I saw her," he said. "She's still with the doctor, but she's going to be okay."

"That's because Joe got her here fast."

"What? Who?"

Patty pointed. "He flies a helicopter and he got her here

faster than me because I got to come in the big truck with the nice lady. The paramedic," she clarified.

The man looked at Joe. "I guess the flight suit should have been a clue. I'm usually more observant."

Joe shrugged. "You've got things on your mind."

The grateful man stuck out his hand. "Thank you."

"You're welcome." Then Joe looked at the little girl. "I have to go, Patty."

"Do you hafta fly other people?" she asked.

"Maybe."

"Thanks for staying with me. It helped me not be so scared."

Joe nodded, then waved and brushed past her. Kate followed, hurrying to keep up with his long stride.

"Wait up," she finally said.

"What for?" he answered, not looking back.

"I want to talk to you."

He slowed, then stopped and turned. "About what?"

"Stuff." She tugged him around the corner into an empty corridor.

"Define *stuff*."

There were so many thoughts running through her head, not to mention emotions in chaos. How did she hammer all that into an articulate list? *Stuff* covered everything.

She said the first thing that popped into her mind. "You're a good man, Joe Morgan."

"Since when?"

"Since you stayed with a terrified little girl. Thanks to you that little girl's mother will get to see her child grow up."

"All I did was fly the chopper. The paramedics and docs here at Mercy Medical worked their magic."

"A team effort, I know. But while they did their trauma thing, you made time for Patty."

"Her mom was relentless. Kept asking how Patty was and said she needed to get to her. All she could think about was her child." He looked down, his feelings shuttered behind a cool blue gaze. "She reminded me of you."

"So you waited for the paramedics to bring Patty in." It wasn't a question.

He shrugged. "I promised I'd make sure she was okay."

"But you could have left. That woman would never have known. The reality is you'll probably never see her or Patty again. But you went out of your way to keep your word. I say again, you're a good man."

He ran his fingers through his hair as he shook his head. Dark intensity pushed through the cool look in his eyes and hinted at a pain deep inside. "There are things you don't know, Kate."

"There are things I do know." She put her hand on his arm and saw something flicker in his expression. "I was wrong not to trust you with J.T. I won't make the mistake again."

"So you're going to let me spend unsupervised time with my son?"

"As much as you want," she confirmed. She nodded once and removed her hand. "He deserves to know his father. Because you *are* a good man."

She started to walk away and felt his strong fingers on her wrist. When he tugged her into his arms, the heat in his eyes stole the air from her lungs.

"If I *were* a good man, I wouldn't have been thinking about this, let alone doing it in a hospital."

He lowered his head and captured her lips with his own. It was a kiss that challenged and tested. Taunted, teased and tempted. Not a sweet, polite kiss. Not even close. His hands were possessive, his mouth greedy. This kiss was just as stunning, shocking and surprising as the first one he'd ever given her and the last one before he'd walked away. But the heat was hotter than she remembered, the wanting more consuming.

When her lips parted instinctively, he took the invitation and ran with it. His tongue swept inside and plundered until she was breathless and weak with need. With one arm an iron band around her waist, he held her to him. Finally, he pulled his mouth from hers and stared down at her, breathing just as hard as she was.

"A nice man wouldn't have done that." He gently cupped her cheek in his big hand. "But just so we're clear, I would never hurt my son. I'd die for him."

"I know," she managed to say.

Before she could say more, he let her go and disappeared around the corner. She touched trembling fingers to her kiss-swollen lips. This time charm had nothing to do with anything. He'd simply taken what he wanted and she'd gone willingly along. There'd been no room for thought about how much it would hurt when he didn't want her any more.

And that time would come. He'd nailed her with the truth. She *was* afraid for herself. Now more than ever she had to find a way to keep her carefully mended heart in one piece.

Chapter Five

How had he screwed up?

Joe looked around Kate's apartment and realized he couldn't count the ways. It looked as if it had been hit by a rocket-propelled grenade, but since he was the only adult present, the blame was all his.

J.T.'s clothes were scattered all over the living room. Some were clean, some not. And he wasn't exactly sure which were which because they'd all merged. It crossed his mind that they were somehow multiplying, although this wasn't the Twilight Zone. It only felt that way. Cars, rattles, baby building blocks and stuffed animals littered every flat surface in the place. Agility and visual acuity were mandatory to successfully negotiate the theater of battle.

The infant seat was on the floor in a holding pattern in case a trip in the car was required. Fat chance. Just keeping his son safe and happy in a contained area was proving to be as much mission as he could handle. Still standing in the middle of the chaos was the baby swing which had been the only thing easy to operate. He was a chopper pilot, after all.

The kitchen was in pretty bad shape, too. There were dishes in the sink, pots on the stove, a coffee cup on the counter. Newspapers on the table he'd actually intended to read. Mission aborted. Sometime before noon he'd intended to straighten up. Sometime after noon he'd gone into survival mode. Kate had called frequently for status reports and he'd assured her everything was secure. Not a lie. He and J.T. were both breathing.

He looked at the baby nestled in his arms, their faces inches apart. "If you were bigger, I'd try to pin the blame for this disaster area on you, pal." J.T. grabbed his nose and laughed. "Right. Your mom would never buy that. If I were you, I'd be careful about trying to put stuff over on her when you get older. In case you don't know it yet, she's a pretty smart cookie."

And hot as Vegas in July.

And if he were counting screwups, number one on the list would be kissing her. Big mistake. All the time he'd been a prisoner, he'd watched and waited, holding back even when bad stuff happened because sometimes that's what a warrior has to do. But she'd stood there in scrubs, looking at him as if he'd just hung the moon and holding back wasn't happening. Her mouth would tempt a saint, and they both knew he was in no danger of going to heaven.

If given half a chance, he didn't trust himself not to do it again. And if she was half as smart as he thought, she wouldn't trust him, either.

She'd told him twice that he was a good man, but she hadn't disagreed when he'd said he wasn't a nice man. Subtle distinction, but she had the scars to prove she understood the difference.

"Your mom may not like me much, pal, but she's a woman

of her word. Or I wouldn't be here watching you while she's at work." Speaking of which... He held the baby up and sniffed. "All clear."

He heard a key in the lock, just before the door opened. Kate walked in with a bag in her hand. She plastered a big fake smile on her face, while her eyes said she needed to see for herself that all was well.

"How's my boy?" she asked, moving closer and planting a big kiss on J.T.

He started kicking his feet and waving his arms.

"I'd say he's glad to see his mom."

She put the bag on the floor, dropped her purse and keys beside it, then took the baby and cuddled him close. "I missed you, Joey T." She looked at him. "Did he miss me?"

"Of course. You were all he talked about."

"Liar." She glanced around. "By the looks of this place, you didn't give him time to miss me."

"Yeah." He ran his fingers through his hair. "About the mess—"

"I was teasing, Joe. It doesn't matter. All I care about is that he's fine. And you survived."

Barely, but she wouldn't hear from him how close he'd been to surrender. "Believe it or not, I did a load of laundry."

"Where is it?" she asked.

"Good question. Best explanation is missing in action. One minute I had piles of clean and piles of dirty. The next, I needed a T-shirt or onesy or shorts or socks and everything sort of became one."

"We'll throw in a load." She shrugged. "No big deal."

"Yes, it is." He folded his arms over his chest. Every muscle in his body ached and he was tired to the bone. "I don't know how you do it by yourself."

"I didn't say it was easy."

"Until today I thought it was. For the record, I'm walking, talking proof that pride goes before a fall."

"Who are you and what have you done with Joe Morgan?" She tipped her head to the side and stared at him. "I like this new and improved attitude."

"A day in the trenches is all it takes." He looked around. "Do you want me to help you straighten up?"

"That's okay. I can do it."

He had no doubt she could. She was pretty amazing and when he looked at her he kept remembering how amazing she tasted. He recalled her softness and how perfectly she fitted against him. It was time to take his attitude out of there.

"I guess I'd better be going."

She put the baby down on the floor blanket, then met his gaze. "Would you like to stay for dinner?"

That was a loaded question if he'd ever heard one. He was afraid to say yes because of how much he wanted to. All he had waiting for him was a huge empty house. Here he could be close to light and warmth. If he said no, he'd risk compromising their tenuous truce.

"It's a simple yes-or-no question," she said. "In case you need something to tip the scales, I stopped at that little Italian place on Arroyo Grande."

"Carlino's?"

"You remember."

He'd never forget. For days and weeks in solitary he'd had nothing but memories of their favorite Italian place with its subdued romantic lighting, candles, flowers on the table and a great bottle of wine. And the best ravioli in tomato cream sauce he'd ever tasted. With Kate looking at him across the table, life had been practically perfect.

"Yeah," he said. "I remember."

"Well, I got takeout." She picked up the bag. "There's enough here for an army."

"I'm a marine."

One who'd kept his sanity in captivity by rereading Kate's letter, remembering the good times and thinking about her and the child they'd made together. He'd watched and waited for an opportunity to escape, then he'd taken it so he could get home to his son, and only his son. He'd walked away from Kate before she could walk away from him. No woman would get a chance to betray him again.

Then he got a grip. This was takeout Italian, not a romantic dinner. It was a negotiating period and he had to meet her halfway.

"I'd like to stay. Thanks."

"I'll set the table." She smiled and for a split second there was no way to protect himself from the radiant warmth. He wanted to fall in and feel it. Then he took a step back.

"What about the little guy?"

"I think you wore him out."

Joe turned and saw that his son was sound asleep, flat on his back on the floor. "Should I put him in his crib?"

She shook her head. "He won't sleep long. When he wakes up I'll give him his dinner and do the bath. Trial and error taught me to seize the occasional quiet moment. Since he was born there haven't been many."

In recent months he'd had moments, but none of them this good.

"Okay," he agreed. "You're the mom."

"You say that as if it's a title with actual authority." She put two placemats on the table, followed by plates, forks and paper napkins.

"After today, I believe you have wings, a halo and you walk on water."

She feigned a look of shock. "Then I'm especially glad I got garlic bread, too."

"With cheese on it?" he asked.

"Duh," she said.

He laughed. "A woman of few words."

She put a container on the bar and folded back the aluminum edges before lifting off the cardboard cover. The aroma of garlic, tomatoes and cheese drifted to him and his stomach growled.

"Did you hear that?" he asked.

She nodded. "I'm guessing you didn't have much chance to eat even though the number of dishes in the sink are evidence to the contrary."

"I think our son has something against the adults around him ingesting food. Do you think he gets that it's counterproductive for his overall well-being?"

"In a word? No." She put a serving spoon in the dish. "Help yourself."

She sat down at a right angle to him and when both plates were filled, started eating. "I'm starved."

"Busy day in the E.R.?"

"Steady. Not overwhelming."

"So it was a good day?" he asked.

"Yeah," she said nodding. "It was a good day."

This was the best day he'd had in a very long time. He'd spent time with his son and nothing out of the ordinary had happened on his watch. Now he was having dinner with a beautiful woman. And when she licked the sauce off her top lip, his day just got a whole lot better. Maybe not better, but definitely hotter. He'd been doing a pretty good job of ignoring the shape and temptation of her mouth until she pulled that maneuver. The mouth that he now knew tasted just the way he'd remembered.

He looked away and forked up a bite of ravioli. *It* tasted just like he remembered, too.

"So," she said, "can we talk about why you're angry with your brother?"

If he'd been drinking, he'd either have choked or spat. There was no doubt he tensed up. "I'd rather not."

"That doesn't surprise me. You're not exactly the great communicator."

"I make exceptions for the important stuff," he said.

"In my opinion this is important."

"Not to me."

"He's J.T.'s uncle. That makes him family."

"An accident of DNA doesn't give him a free pass."

"What does that mean?" she prodded.

"Once a bastard, always a bastard. You pointed out that it's your job to protect J.T. As his father, I have the same responsibility. It's better for him if he doesn't know my brother."

"Is it possible you're overreacting?"

"No."

Silence stretched out between them as she waited for more. She'd have to wait till hell froze. Preston Morgan was dead to him.

"That's it?" she asked.

"It's enough."

And just like that the ambience was gone and it ticked him off that his brother still had the power to take something away from him. But maybe he'd dodged a bullet. Now he was remembering how it felt to be betrayed instead of thinking about kissing Kate. Since he didn't want to be at risk ever again, that was probably for the best.

* * *

While J.T. played in his crib, Kate put bottles in the diaper bag and checked the rest of the supplies always stocked in it. Diapers, wipes, powder and cream. Check.

She stood by the sofa and shook her head. "This isn't a good idea, Joe."

"You're right."

That was way too easy, she thought. "I'm glad you agree."

"It's not a good idea. It's great."

"For us to do something together?" she questioned.

He put his hands on his hips. In snug black T-shirt, worn jeans and boots, he was about the sexiest man ever. And he wanted to spend the day together with her and J.T. She should count her lucky stars he wasn't suggesting spending the night.

"I've been home for six weeks now, Kate. Either I'm working or you are and the other one is with the baby. Today we both have the day off and it's time we did something. The three of us. Together as a unit."

She tilted her head and sent him a suspicious look. "You're not taking us on a forced march, are you?"

"Payback for baby boot camp?" He grinned and shook his head. "Nah. The thought never occurred to me."

That meant this was probably about bonding as a family unit. Kate wasn't going after clarification about her suspicion. It was a minefield she didn't even want to step in. As far as she was concerned, they were bonded enough. Doing extracurricular stuff wasn't part of her plan and her plan was all about not falling for Joe. But she didn't see any way to get out of this day trip gracefully.

She had to acknowledge that if a tiny part of her wasn't looking forward to spending the day with him, she wouldn't care about graceful. She would have simply said no. She'd managed to do that when he'd had the insane idea of getting married, but today that single-syllable word hadn't come out of her mouth. That spoke volumes.

The day he'd comforted a little girl at the hospital he'd said he wasn't a nice man. She'd agreed because a nice man wouldn't have led her on, then dropped her like a hot rock. But he was different now. He did all the things a nice man would do. That was the man who could do her the most harm.

"Where are you taking us?" she asked.

"It's a surprise," he answered mysteriously. "Is J.T. ready?"

She nodded. "Just waiting to go in the car seat."

"I'll get him."

She was grateful. The baby was almost six months old and growing so fast. He was deadweight, especially in the car seat, yet Joe toted him easily. Moments later he held the handle of the seat and the muscles in his arm bunched and stretched the sleeve of his T-shirt.

He'd been a little thin when he'd showed up at her place six weeks ago. Since that night the man had filled out in all the right places. His shoulders were wide, strong, the kind a girl could lean on. Except Kate knew that wasn't true.

She followed him to the lot where he'd parked the expensive SUV he'd recently purchased. She had no idea which model it was, but knew any of the luxury models were beyond her budget. And the cost didn't make it any less a *family* vehicle. He was putting on quite the show. She had a front-row seat and had to resist getting sucked into the illusion.

Joe secured J.T. in the back, then got behind the wheel while she fastened her seat belt. After sliding on his aviator sunglasses, he looked at her and smiled. It was a good look—masculine and sexy. It was a look that made normal breathing a challenge. It was a look that reminded her why this outing was such a bad idea.

"Ready?" he asked.

"As I'll ever be."

He pulled out of the apartment complex, then turned onto Green Valley Parkway to the 215 Beltway and headed toward the 15 Freeway north, passing the Las Vegas Strip. Mandalay Bay, Excalibur, Bellagio and Caesar's Palace were on her right. It was a unique skyline during the day, and really spectacular lit up at night. They called this city the most exciting place on the planet and for her lately it had lived up to the hype.

She glanced in the back seat and saw that J.T. had fallen asleep, as he usually did in the car. The silence was louder than usual and she couldn't think of anything to say to break it.

Sharing baby duty had become natural. But now, in the intimacy of the car, she was so acutely aware of Joe, the way he smelled, his silhouette all masculine angles, his big hands so confident on the steering wheel…. She couldn't shake the feeling of wanting those hands all over her in the most intimate possible way. It was just like the first time she'd seen him.

Actually, it was worse, even more acute than the first time. Then she'd fallen into his bed. Now she was determined not to. It would be a lot easier if she didn't keep thinking about that kiss at the hospital. The memory cranked up the heat and started a need that wouldn't go away.

Just because the emotions were constantly simmering didn't mean she had to give in. That would be the mistake. Some of Kate's earliest memories were of her mother's men. Even now Candy hadn't learned to keep from being hurt. The thing about hurt was that it rolled downhill and no one around you got off scot-free. Kate was free of it now and determined not to put J.T. in a painful situation.

"You're awfully quiet over there," Joe said, glancing at her. "Anything I should know about?"

"No. Just wondering where we're going."

Joe exited the freeway at Rancho Drive and headed north past numerous strip malls, bars and grills and local casinos. Just before Decatur Boulevard, he made a right turn into the North Las Vegas airport.

"It's a clue," she said.

"This is where I work." He glanced at her. "I wanted to show you."

She could read a whole lot of personal stuff into that statement and the quiver in her stomach told her she already had. But her mind wasn't going there. Not willingly.

"I'd like to see it," she said.

It was an industrial complex with big, corrugated metal buildings scattered over a wide area. A shadow moved over the car and she glanced out the window as a small plane passed overhead, coming in for a landing.

Joe turned left, and headed for the far end. There were several helicopters parked by a hangar. One said Police Rescue, and the other had a logo from a local news channel. Then he pulled into a space by a two-story beige building that bore a sign reading Southwestern Helicopter Service.

"This is the office. Over there behind it is the hangar where the mechanics work on the choppers. We sublease equipment to the police and fire departments, and companies that fly tours to the Grand Canyon. Here's where we do the maintenance and repairs."

He unbuckled the car seat and lifted the still-sleeping baby out of the car. "Come on. I'll introduce you to a couple of the guys."

She grabbed the diaper bag, then followed him across the blacktop and into the shade of the hangar. A big fan in the corner blew the hot air around while two men—one blond, the other dark-haired, both dressed in blue coveralls—bent over small, oil-covered, mysterious pieces of machinery.

Joe stopped just inside the wide opening. "Hey, guys."

The two men turned, their gazes skimming over her and the baby. Then they smiled and said, "Hi, boss."

"Skip, Wes, this is Kate Carpenter."

She lifted her hand in a wave. "Hi."

The blond man stood and walked over. "I'm Wes. This must be your little guy," he said, smiling down at the baby.

"Yeah," Joe said, a tender look filled with pride on his face.

"Cute."

"Thanks."

Skip, short and stocky, wiped his greasy hands on an orange rag and joined them. "How old is he?"

"Almost six months," Kate answered.

"You got a big one there," the dark-haired man said. "My little guy is almost a year now and he's about the same size."

"What's your son's name?" Kate asked.

"Henry." Skip shrugged. "Family name on my wife's side."

"It's a good strong name," she said.

"You're planning to stop in the office," Wes said. It wasn't a question. "Laura will never let you hear the end of it if you don't show her the baby."

"I figured," Joe said. "We're going there now."

"Nice to meet you, Kate," Skip said.

"You, too." She smiled then turned to follow Joe. "Who's Laura?"

"The office manager. She's been here ever since I can remember. Since my father started the company."

"So she knows where in the closet all your skeletons are," she said.

He glanced at her sharply, then looked away. "I have no skeletons."

"If you say so."

A bell tinkled when Joe opened the office door, then he stepped back and let her precede him into the air-conditioned interior. Metal desks, one behind the other, filled the open space. Black-and-white photographs of airplanes and helicopters lined the walls.

An older woman, short and blond, walked into the room. She was chewing and had a napkin in her hand. Finally she said, "It's just you."

"This is Laura Bunker," he said. "As you can tell from that comment, she's in awe of me."

She ignored him and held out her hand to Kate, blue eyes twinkling. "Pleased to meet you."

"Kate Carpenter," Kate said, squeezing the other woman's fingers.

"So this is the baby you've been bragging so much about." She bent and studied J.T., smiling tenderly. "Oh, Joe, no wonder you're so proud. He's a handsome little guy. I see some of your father in him." She straightened and looked at Kate. "His father hired me because of my last name—Bunker. Said it sounded military enough for a retired marine."

"So," Kate said, glancing at Joe. "You followed in your father's military footsteps and joined up?"

"More like he was shoved in that direction," Laura said. "Joe was a challenge when he was a teenager. After that incident—" She stopped at the warning expression on his face and grinned. "Suffice it to say his father thought the Marine Corps would give him some structure and discipline."

"And did it?" Kate asked.

"I found helicopters and caught flying fever." He shrugged.

"Your father must have been proud."

"If he was," Joe said, "he never told me."

"Doesn't mean he didn't feel it." Laura folded her arms over her ample breasts. "He was a man of few words."

"At the risk of borrowing trouble," Kate said, glancing out the window at the helicopters parked a hundred yards away. "Just so we're clear, J.T. isn't going to become a pilot in order to earn your affection. He will always know how you feel about him because you'll freely express your pride in his accomplishments."

He saluted. "Yes, ma'am."

"He's ma'aming me." She sighed. "I can't speak from personal experience, but common sense dictates that open communication between family members should—"

Laura snapped her fingers. "Speaking of family, you just missed Preston."

There was an uncomfortable silence before Joe asked, "What was he doing here?"

"Checking on things."

"Since when?"

"Since he owns half the company. You changed your day off at the last minute. He wanted to talk to you."

"Then I guess I got lucky." The harshness in Joe's voice could strip rust off a trailer hitch.

Laura's eyes narrowed on him. "If you want my opinion, it's time you two talked about things and buried the hatchet."

"Not likely," Joe said.

"Whatever." The older woman's mouth pulled tight for a moment. "You're as stubborn as your dad. So is Preston." She shook her head and threw up her hands. "But I'm not getting involved. I'm entitled to a lunch break and I plan to finish mine in the break room. Kate, it was nice to meet you and your little guy."

"You, too," she said.

The other woman walked to the doorway in the rear of the room and disappeared inside, slamming the door behind her.

Kate remembered the last time the subject of his brother had come up. He'd been angry then, too, and she'd felt badly about messing up the teasing banter between them. Today wasn't her fault. But she'd have to be deaf, dumb and blind not to see that this rift was eating away at him and she agreed with Laura. Whatever was bothering him needed to be aired.

She wasn't his employee. She wasn't sure what she was to him, except the mother of his child. That should count for something.

She looked up at him. "What happened between you and your brother?"

"Nothing."

"Oh? Apparently your office manager has quite an opinion about that nothing."

"Laura has an opinion about everything." He looked down at the car seat because the baby started to cry.

"She's been here a long time and knows you both pretty well. It obviously concerns her if she mentioned it in front of me."

"Nothing's going on. Forget about it." He squatted and lifted J.T. into his arms. The little guy was always grumpy after a car-seat nap which effectively ended the conversation. Lucky for Joe since he didn't want to have it in the first place.

When J.T. held out his arms to her, she took him and cuddled him close. The angry, lost expression on Joe's face made her want to do the same thing to him. So much for family day.

The thing was, Preston Morgan was J.T.'s uncle, which made *him* family. For a girl who'd never had family, it seemed a shame to throw a perfectly good one away. Whether Joe liked it or not, they were going to have a conversation about why he treated his brother as if he were a particularly virulent and deadly strain of the plague.

Chapter Six

There was a small terminal in the airport and upstairs on the second floor was a coffee shop called Wings 'n Things. After Kate settled J.T. down, Joe took them there for lunch. They had a booth with a window where they could look out and watch small to mid-sized planes taking off, helicopters coming and going. All of this activity played out against the backdrop of the craggy Nevada mountains in the distance.

North Las Vegas Airport was convenient to the Strip, about twenty minutes away. It was nowhere near as big as McCarran and that made it hassle-free, but at the rate the valley was growing that wouldn't be the case for long.

Speaking of hassles, Joe was pretty sure there was one in his very immediate future. He wished Laura hadn't mentioned Preston's visit, or at least that she had waited until Kate wasn't present. Judging by the confusion, uncertainty and, finally, determination in her expression, she was going to start asking questions.

Right now she was busy wiping J.T.'s high-chair tray with one of the disinfectant wipes she kept in the diaper bag. Then she put small circles of cereal on the germ-free tray—for small motor development as well as eye-hand coordination, Kate had once explained. And to keep him busy so she could eat in peace.

He passed Kate one of the menus tucked behind the salt, pepper and condiments. She opened hers and scanned the three pages. When she closed it, the thirtyish dark-haired waitress, wearing a T-shirt sporting the Wings 'n Things logo of a small plane, stopped at their table.

She smiled and crooked a one-finger wave at the baby. "Hi, cutie." He smiled, and she looked at him, then at Kate. "I'm Barbara. I'll be your server today. What can I get you?"

"Iced tea," Joe said.

Kate nodded. "Me, too."

After jotting that down, Barbara said, "Have you made up your mind? Or do you need a minute?"

"I'll have the Wild Bleu Yonder burger with fries," Kate said. "And extra bleu cheese."

Joe closed his menu. "Good choice. I'll have the same."

Barbara looked from one to the other. "If you two are always this compatible, life at your house must be pretty quiet."

"Not always." Kate smiled but there was an edge to it. "You could call this the calm before the storm."

"Okay, then. I'll be back with your drinks." Barbara walked away and quickly returned with the iced tea, then discreetly disappeared.

Kate looked around. "This place is very aviator-oriented."

"Location, location, location," he said wryly.

"Yeah. I get that. It's really cool with all the pictures of airplanes and the airport in the 1930s."

On the wall beside her there was a frame with a poem in it. She read out loud, "'Someday we will know where the pilots go when their work on earth is through. Where the air is clean and their engines gleam and the skies are always blue.'" She met his gaze and her own was soft before she started reading again. "'They have flown alone with the engine's moan as they sweat the great beyond. Yet not alone for above the moan when the earth is out of sight, He takes their hand and guides them through the night. And how they live and love and are beloved, but their love is most for air. And with death about they still fly out and leave their troubles there. He knows these things of men and wings, and He knows they are surely true. And He will give a hand to such a man 'cause He's a pilot, too.'"

Her voice broke and tears glittered in her eyes when she finished. "Poignant and profound," she said huskily.

"Yeah."

"You told me once that in your opinion anyone who doesn't want to fly is crazy."

"I remember."

He remembered, too, the first time they'd met. It had been at the hospital when he cut his hand. One look at her and the pain had disappeared. He'd taken her to dinner after her E.R. shift, then taken her to bed. After making love to her, he'd held her and talked about how much flying helicopters meant to him. He'd learned a lot since then about what's really important.

"Do you believe God is your copilot?"

Joe put out his finger and let J.T. grab it as he met her gaze across the table. "If He wasn't, I wouldn't be here now."

They made small talk until their food order arrived and Kate

ate half of hers before commenting. "This is the best hamburger I've had in a really long time."

"It's good," Joe agreed. "But I have to say— You need to get out more."

"If I promise to do that, will you tell me what's going on with you and your brother?"

It was too much to hope she'd forgotten, or would simply give him a pass. "Look, Kate, do you really want to spoil a family day out with ancient history?"

She wiped her mouth with a paper napkin. "That's the thing. It's not ancient. I could tell by your reaction that it's still very current."

He ate a couple of fries as he studied her, the stubborn glint in her eyes that told him dodging the question wasn't an option. He'd have to throw her a bone. "Preston and I don't like each other much." Even before his brother had slept with his wife they hadn't been close.

Kate put more cereal out for J.T. and his smooth brow furrowed in concentration as he struggled to pick the pieces up. "Why?"

"It's a sibling thing."

"I never had one, so you're going to have to explain it to me."

He blew out a long breath as he wadded up his napkin and tossed it on his plate. "As far as my father was concerned Preston was the golden boy and I was a royal screwup."

"Why did he think that?"

"Could have happened when the cops called him after arresting me."

Her eyes grew wide. "What did you do?"

"Which time?"

"There was more than one?"

"Yeah."

He'd had a lot of time to think about this, too. When he was going through it, he'd believed the worst about himself. He didn't know how much more he was capable of until joining the Corps. Now he just wanted to forget that stupid, sowing-wild-oats teenage stuff along with a few grown-up mistakes.

"Do you want to tell me about it?"

"No." Before she could ask another question, he said, "My father strongly encouraged me to sign up for military service. I got the it-worked-for-me-and-is-just-what-you-need lecture."

"So you did follow in his footsteps," Kate observed.

"In a manner of speaking."

She leaned over and kissed J.T.'s cheek. "That means there's a very real possibility this innocent little boy has a DNA disposition to being a troublemaker based on the history of his grandfather and his father."

"I suppose you could say that." Joe shrugged. "Although we had a talk and I advised him not to try and put anything over on you."

"Thanks for that." She smiled and picked up the white paper that covered her straw and started to shred it. "Did your brother ever get arrested?"

"Are you serious? Perfect Preston?" The sarcasm didn't take the knot out of his gut as he'd hoped. Maybe nothing ever would. And not because his brother was a tough act to follow. It had to do with the fact that he wouldn't trust the bastard as far as he could throw him. "He's a lawyer now. But you already know that if you went to his office."

She studied him intently. "What aren't you telling me?"

"A lot, in the interest of time."

"That's not what I meant and I think you know it. You're not telling me something."

How the hell did she know that? She was right, but there were parts of the past that he wasn't willing to talk about and that was one. It had no bearing on anything relevant to his son and life now. It was available on a need-to-know basis and she didn't need to know.

"Kate, just drop it. We share the business because my father left it to us both and neither would sell out. Preston handles the legal end and I do the day-to-day stuff." He ran his fingers through his hair. "And one more thing."

"What?" she asked.

"I have a good reason for feeling the way I do. I'd appreciate it if you'd respect that. Just take my word for it."

"I respect your word."

Joe nodded as relief swelled through him. Even though there was nothing between them but a child, the thought of his brother coming on to Kate made him crazy. It wasn't about being jealous. It was about doing his job, which was protecting the mother of his son. Preston had already fouled one relationship. Joe didn't intend to let him anywhere near Kate.

"Thank you for seeing me without an appointment, Mr. Morgan—"

"As I recall, the last time you came to see me I asked you to call me Preston."

"All right. Preston." Kate settled the strap of her purse more securely on her shoulder. "I appreciate this very much."

"Please sit down," he said, indicating one of the chairs in front of his desk.

"All right." She sat on the edge, an appropriate place to be since she was on edge and walking a fine line.

If Joe knew she was here… Well, he wouldn't be happy. And that was the mother of all understatements.

She'd been pregnant the last time she'd been here—the only time. And it looked the same. Preston Morgan's office was located in a business complex on Eastern Avenue, not far from Mercy Medical Center. It was elegantly appointed with mahogany office furniture, leather chairs and a sofa in the waiting room covered in green microfiber material. As far as art, she didn't know a watercolor from an oil, but Kate had a feeling the paintings on the walls were pricey. And the glass vases and bowls displayed in the corner armoire of Preston Morgan's personal space were not meant to hold leftovers from dinner.

She studied Joe's brother who also looked the same as last time. Well dressed, although the long sleeves of his white dress shirt were rolled to the elbow in work mode. The red power tie was loose at his collar. He had black hair and intense blue eyes, apparently a Morgan family trait. Preston was a good-looking man just like his brother. But the edgy charisma that she'd first noticed about Joe, the excitement that attracted her to him, was missing. At least for her.

Preston was sitting behind his desk, watching her, waiting for her to say something.

"I'm sorry. I was just remembering the last time I was here," she explained.

She'd been curious about Joe then, too. Had needed information about him just like she did now. She'd still been hurting from his sudden rejection even though several months had passed. Then he'd ignored her letter about being pregnant, which had hammered her emotions again. It hadn't been his fault, but the pain of rejection had been very real and a lesson in how much he could hurt her if she wasn't careful.

"You're not pregnant any more," Preston pointed out.

She looked down. "The last time my lap was rapidly disappearing."

He smiled. "In a most charming way."

"If you like the beached-whale look."

"You wore it well," he said.

"You're incredibly diplomatic."

"So what brings you here this time?" he asked. "You're not trying to find Joe again?"

She shook her head. "He came to see me when he got back to the States. I know he was a prisoner of war. Now we're— We have—" She struggled to find the words to explain what they had. A passionate past. Heat that didn't show signs of cooling off any time soon. An attraction that became more difficult to ignore every time she saw him. Mutual respect. They shared a child and were probably the most dysfunctional family on the planet. Finally she said, "He wants to be a father to his son. We have an understanding."

One corner of his mouth curved up. "How's that working for you?"

"It could be better."

"Oh?" He leaned back in his chair and linked his fingers over his flat abdomen. "It doesn't take a mental giant to deduce that you think I can help somehow."

"Right. Otherwise I wouldn't be here. On my lunch break." Because she didn't want Joe to know about this visit.

"So what can I do for you, Kate?"

She met his gaze. "You can tell me what's going on between you and Joe."

A flicker of a frown flashed across his face then disappeared. "My brother and I are partners in Southwestern Helicopter."

"I'm aware of that. And it seems to be the only part of the relationship that's working."

"Did you ask Joe about this?"

"Yes. Now I'd like your side of it." She was bluffing, and hoped he'd bite and give her the 411.

He blew out a long breath. "What did he tell you?"

"That you're not close."

"I see."

He was such an attorney, not giving anything away. She was going to have to work for this. Twenty questions, starting now. "Do you feel the same way?"

"Sibling relationships are often complicated."

"That's not an answer, Preston."

"I'm aware of that. I'm just trying to figure out why your understanding with my brother spills over into trying to figure me out."

"And I'd tell you that if I could." Joe was there for his son which was all that should concern her. Except the dynamic of his bond with his brother could be relevant to J.T. some day. She sensed that Joe was in pain, angry, and it was more than simply about sibling rivalry and competing for their father's affection. "It's complicated."

"What we have here is a standoff."

"I'd like to understand what's going on."

His gaze narrowed on her. "Did Joe send you here?"

"Would that make a difference?"

"Maybe."

"Why?"

"It's complicated," he said, parroting her words. He sighed as a faraway expression settled in his eyes. There was melancholy there, too, as if he'd been hoping.

"Do you miss your brother?" she asked.

"It's hard to miss what you never had." He leaned forward and rested his forearms on the papers scattered over his desk top.

"But you'd like to change that." It wasn't a question.

"It seems as if Joe and I have always been at odds."

"He told me your father always liked you best," she said.

"That's not the way it looked from where I was standing."

"Care to explain that?"

He shrugged. "Dad talked about Joe all the time. The son who was serving his country. Flew helicopters. Saved lives in a theater of war. A hero."

"So he was proud of Joe?"

"You could say that." He laughed, but there was no humor in it. "In his eyes there was no greater calling than a career in the Corps."

"Why didn't he say all this to Joe?"

"That's a good question. Military mentality. Compliments make you soft. Different generation. The Morgan method of parenting. Take your pick."

She studied the sadness and longing in his eyes and realized Joe wasn't the only one who had craved his father's respect, admiration and love. Preston had gone through a tough upbringing, too. Only someone who'd gone through the experience could understand. The two brothers needed to talk and she had a feeling Preston wanted to.

"You and Joe need to have a beer together."

He stared at her, then laughed. "Don't tell me. You believe in Santa Claus, the Easter Bunny and happy endings, too."

"Make fun if you want, but the sarcasm in that response tells me I hit a nerve."

"And that response tells me to rest my case."

In lawyer speak that was a big clue that he wouldn't say more. She wasn't going to get any information out of him, which was another Morgan family trait, and not an especially attractive one from her perspective.

"I've taken up enough of your time, Preston. I have to get back to the hospital."

"How's the baby?"

"Perfect." She smiled. "Would you like to see a picture?"

"Very much."

She pulled out her wallet and handed it across his desk, opened to several pictures of J.T. "He'll be six months old next week. He's almost crawling and I have no doubt he's the most gifted child ever born."

Preston studied the photos from newborn to current. He met her gaze. "He looks like Joe."

When he handed it back, Kate studied the picture. "He has my chin."

"Maybe."

His tone said he was humoring her. She looked closer and saw that the baby's grin and blue eyes were all Joe. Dark hair the same shade as his father's drifted over his forehead. There was even a small indentation in his chin, hardly more than a shadow, that he'd inherited from the Morgan side of the family.

The thing was she'd known this all along. If she'd never seen Joe again, the baby would still have been an ever-present reminder of the man she'd cared so much about. The man who had taken her feelings and handed them back to her before walking out of her life.

"You're right. He looks nothing like me."

He stood. "I didn't say that."

"Not in so many words." She rose and slung her purse strap over her shoulder. "But there's little question that he favors the Morgan side of the family."

"Yeah. I can't believe I've never seen my nephew," he said, resting his hands on lean hips. "At least not on this side of the womb."

"He looks much better now."

"I'm sure." He glanced down, then met her gaze. "I'd like to see him. If that's okay with *you*."

She got the inflection and knew he was saying that Joe

wouldn't be happy. And she was conflicted about that. The bottom line was that she wanted her son to have the family she'd never had, and his Uncle Preston was part of it.

"That would be fine. After all, you're his uncle."

"Thanks."

"No problem."

Preston looked at her for several moments, then said, "Does Joe have any idea that you're in love with him?"

"Now who's making up fairy tales?" She felt as if he'd hit her in the chest with a baseball bat and hoped her comeback covered the shock. "I never had time to know how deep my feelings went before he broke things off."

"And now?" Preston pushed.

"Now we're exhausted working parents and there's no energy for love."

"My mistake." But his expression said he wasn't so sure about that.

Shaken, she said goodbye, then left the office. She wasn't in love with Joe. That's not why she'd gone to see his brother. She'd told herself it was for her son, and she hoped she wasn't lying.

In spite of that off-the-mark observation, Kate saw no reason to discourage J.T.'s uncle. In her experience too many men walked away from responsibility. Not the Morgan men. They seemed to embrace it, exceptions to the rule. More important, they were both J.T.'s family.

But Uncle Preston had planted a disturbing thought in her mind. No way was she falling for Joe again.

Chapter Seven

"That man has the bedside manner of a Neanderthal." Kate was fuming as she walked from the E.R. to the cafeteria with her best friend.

"I can't argue with that." Sandy Richardson hurried to keep up. "But he's really good at what he does."

"I know that. I respect his abilities as a doctor. As a human being?" She angrily shook her head. "Not so much."

Redheaded Sandy sighed. "You have to admit that people can be, shall we diplomatically say, lacking in common sense. The patient shot himself in the leg with a nail gun, Kate."

"Still, Dr. Tenney didn't have to make that poor man feel like he was gum stuck to the bottom of his shoe."

They turned left and walked past the Respiratory Therapy department, then made another left, skirting the lobby and following the hallway toward the smell of food. And coffee. Kate desperately needed a cup. The night before J.T. had slept fitfully, therefore she had, too.

The cafeteria was at the end of the hall. A large open room, it had oak-trimmed tables placed in the center where the ceiling rose into the bell tower visible from the exterior. Through an archway was another room with more seating. Bulletin boards hung on the walls with notices of upcoming employee activities and a nutrition corner displaying heart-healthy recipes. Kate and Sandy got into the steam table line. Across the way was the hot- and cold-drink dispenser.

"Think about it from Tenney's perspective, Kate." Sandy's big green eyes sparkled with mischief. Sometimes she took way too much pleasure in playing devil's advocate. "He sees stuff like that nail-gun incident all the time. People being careless. Did you know his brother died in the E.R. a while back?"

"No." Kate looked at her sharply. "What happened? Was Mitch working when they brought him in?"

"I don't know any details." Sandy shook her head. "It happened a couple of years ago, before we started working here."

The two of them had gone through orientation together, huddled together like motherless monkeys, and bonded in the E.R. where they both worked. Kate didn't think she'd have gotten through the emotional ups and downs of the last two years without her friend.

Each built a meal from all the choices on the salad bar, then grabbed a soda and filed past the cashier. In unspoken agreement, they chose a table around the corner from the coffee dispenser.

Kate sat down. "Who told you about Mitch's brother?"

"Rhonda. She's been the E.R. manager so long, she knows everyone's secrets."

Not mine, Kate thought. No one knew she'd gone to see Joe's brother except his brother. Therefore, her secret was safe.

"I'm sorry about his loss," Kate said. "But you'd think that would make him more sympathetic to people."

"Maybe something stupid cost him a loved one." At Kate's look, Sandy shrugged. "I'm just saying…"

"Has it ever occurred to you that I might simply want to be ticked off at the guy?"

"What guy?" Joe stood beside them in all his masculine flight-gear glory. Obviously he'd just brought in a patient.

Kate's heart started to pound. "It's nothing."

"The E.R. doc," Sandy said. "She's mad at him."

"I could beat him up for you," Joe offered.

Sandy grinned at her before glancing up. "It's not every day a girl gets an offer like that. When a hero comes along…"

Been there, done that. Still had the scars to prove it, Kate thought.

"As appealing as that offer is, violence is not the answer." Kate noticed the lidded cup in his hand. "I guess you're leaving?"

"I've got a minute." He set the drink on the table and sat between them.

Sandy looked puzzled as she glanced at him. "Who are you?"

Kate couldn't believe they'd never met. Then the memories of their hot affair flooded back. She and Joe had only had eyes for each other and spent every minute together alone. Very alone. Wrapped in each other's arms. Very naked.

She cleared her throat. "Sandy, this is Joe Morgan. Joe, Sandy Richardson, my best friend."

"Nice to meet you," he said.

The thermostat on Sandy's expression dropped into the icy range.

Kate had told her friend everything. Falling for Joe and him abruptly ending it. She knew he was J.T.'s father and had come back from Afghanistan. She knew all the good, bad and ugly. And it felt good to have someone in her corner.

"So *you're* Joe Morgan."

"Guilty." He looked at Kate. "How's J.T.?"

"Fine. I dropped him off at Marilyn's this morning and I've checked in. He's napping and being an angel."

He nodded. "He gets that angelic thing from you."

"I'm no angel."

"Well, he doesn't get it from me." For a split second there was a haunted look in his eyes.

"Time will tell. But he most definitely looks like you. Even his—" She stopped just before the word *uncle* came out of her mouth. Preston had noticed the resemblance, but that wasn't something she wanted to share. It was a can of worms best left sealed up tight.

"What?"

"Nothing. Just that he's got your eyes and hair. The girls are going to be after him before we know it."

"Not a problem. As long he slows down enough for a girl like his mother to catch him."

Kate stared at him. "Hey, flyboy. Was there an incident in the chopper? Oxygen interruption?"

"I don't go high enough to need oxygen. What's your point?" The corners of his mouth turned up in a look designed to weaken knees and melt hearts.

"Oh, please," Sandy muttered.

"My point is," Kate said, glancing at her friend, "who hit you with the flattery stick?"

"I'm just telling the truth." Suddenly he reached for the pager in his jumpsuit pocket and looked at the display. He stood and picked up his coffee. "Gotta go. See you after work, Kate?"

"Okay."

She watched him walk out and the sight of his wide shoulders and narrow waist, the masculine sight of Joe in a jumpsuit, just made her warm clear through.

"So," Sandy said, "the next sound you hear will be fire alarms going off."

"What?" Kate dragged her gaze from the empty doorway.

"You. Joe. Sparks. Fire." One auburn eyebrow rose. "I don't think you've mentioned that you still have the hots for him."

"Because I don't." Kate picked up her fork and started eating, even though her appetite had disappeared.

"This is me, buddy. I was there to pick up the pieces after he broke your heart. I listened when every day went by and he didn't respond to the news that he was going to be a father—"

"That wasn't his fault."

Sandy held up a hand. "I'm aware of that. It still doesn't change the fact that you believed he didn't want you or his child. I remember how much it hurt even if you don't."

"How could I forget?" Kate couldn't argue with the truth. She met her friend's concerned gaze and said, "But he's Joe."

"Yeah. So I saw." Sandy glanced at the doorway where he'd disappeared. "He wouldn't have to wear a bag over his head in public. But looks aren't everything."

"It isn't just that. How shallow do you think I am?"

"This is me," Sandy said again, grinning this time. "Unlike chopper Joe, I know you're not an angel."

"Okay. I'll admit some susceptibility to those eyes and the smile. But you said it yourself. When a hero comes along… He's doing all the right things. Being a father to J.T. He even asked me to marry him—"

"He what?" Sandy's hand froze with her fork halfway between her plate and her mouth. "You never told me that."

"Really?" Kate played dumb. It wasn't difficult. Where Joe

was concerned she was the planet's biggest pea brain. That proposal wasn't something she'd wanted to talk about. Now the cat was out of the bag. "When he got back. Right after he saw J.T. for the first time. He said we should get married."

"And you said?"

"No, of course." Now she wasn't so sure about the adamant "of course" part. "But—"

"What?" Her friend wore a wary expression. Sandy did cynical better than anyone besides Kate.

"The thing is, I'm having trouble remembering why I was so angry with him."

Sandy chewed her last bite of salad, then washed it down with a sip of diet soda. "Let me remind you then. He flew in, swept you off your feet with his dashing pilot act, then without any warning said, 'Oops, just kidding. It's not working for me,' and walked out."

"Yeah, but—"

"No but," Sandy said. "Don't tell me that was before he knew about J.T. The thing is that's a measure of who he is. Pure and simple. Nothing complicated to muck it up. If the relationship isn't solid, staying together for a child's sake won't work."

Kate sighed. "He kissed me, Sandy."

Her friend's eyes grew wide. "Surely you mean before. When you were going hot and heavy. Not now."

"No. I mean now. Since he came back."

"Where?"

"Here in the hospital. In a corner—"

Sandy shook her head. "No. I mean where on you? The cheek? Your hand?"

"Nope. Lips and lots of tongue."

Sandy groaned. "Tell me it did nothing for you."

"I could tell you that," Kate said, "but it would be a big fat lie."

"And you didn't tell me before now because?"

Kate pushed salad around her plate without meeting her friend's eyes. "Because I already knew what you'd say. And you're right." She looked up. "But this is what I can't seem to get out of my head. What if he had a really good reason for dumping me?"

"What reason could there possibly be if he truly cared about you?"

"I don't know. But I judged him unfairly when he didn't respond to my letter. Maybe I should give him the benefit of the doubt. What if there's a chance for a do-over?"

"What if he breaks your heart again? What if he leaves you and his son again? He did it once. You know he's capable."

"I have to admit the thought occurred to me." More precisely, the thought was never far from her mind. "But I can't help wondering 'what if.' You know?"

"Yeah, I do know." Sandy sighed and shadows darkened her eyes to hazel. "Nothing hurts more than wondering about what might have been."

Kate's curiosity was definitely aroused by *that* comment, but her friend blew off questions and finally said she had to get back to work. After watching the other nurse walk out, Kate filled a to-go cup with coffee as thoughts tumbled through her mind. Obviously her best friend had a lot in common with Joe.

They both had secrets.

If Sandy didn't want to share, that was her business. No harm, no foul. But Joe didn't have that luxury. He was the father of her son and, to his credit, insisted on being there for J.T. It was her job to learn about him. Not for herself. For their son. She'd survived heartbreak once and knew how to protect herself now. But J.T. was innocent and not even his father had the right to do him wrong.

Her job was to protect her little man at the same time she protected her heart from the other man in her life.

Kate stared over the candle on the table in Hugo's Cellar, a romantic restaurant in the Four Queens Hotel. "You had help pulling this off."

"I'm a marine. I don't need help."

Joe considered his military background a source of pride. The traditions of the Corps and specialized training he'd received had helped get him through the worst in Afghanistan. So had thoughts of Kate and the son he had so badly wanted to live long enough to see.

But he was teasing her about not needing help. Arranging this evening out—just the two of them—had been an undertaking not unlike deploying personnel and equipment halfway around the world during the First Gulf War. He was definitely dressed better now. The charcoal suit and coordinating tie with splashes of red were new. He was glad he'd gone the extra mile because Kate looked amazing. Earlier, when he'd first seen her in her brief, black dress, his tongue had stuck to the roof of his mouth. Now here they were, drinking champagne.

She took a sip from her flute, her eyes sparkling as brightly as the bubbles in her glass. "If Marilyn hadn't agreed to keep J.T., the whole operation would have been blown. That constitutes help, even for a marine."

"Child care doesn't count."

Her eyes twinkled. "I refuse to argue the finer points with you." Then her smile disappeared. "No one's ever surprised me like this."

"Because there wasn't a marine planning the mission."

She shook her head. "No one ever tried."

Somehow he didn't think that was a good thing. The hint of

sadness lurking in her eyes was a clue. But sadness wasn't an option. Not tonight. It was about celebrating.

"But you were surprised?" he asked.

"Completely," she confirmed.

"Mission accomplished."

Somewhere between their family outing and seeing her at the hospital he'd come up with the idea of taking her to dinner. He wanted to believe it had nothing to do with her friend Sandy looking at him as if he had single-handedly saved the world one minute, and as if he were the world's most prolific serial killer the next.

He'd known right then that Kate had confided their complicated history to her friend. Something else came to mind. He'd never thanked Kate for giving him a son. It's what this dinner was all about.

Mostly.

But he didn't want to put a finer point on his motivation. Their past *was* complicated. The thing about history was that studying it helped avoid the same mistakes in the future.

Kate had thought about keeping J.T. from him. So noted. Information tucked away in his emotional perimeter. That didn't mean their son's mother and father couldn't enjoy an evening of R & R.

"I still can't believe you dropped J.T. off with Marilyn."

"She agreed to watch him, but it had to be at her place because she had a previous obligation to keep her granddaughter."

"She's certainly in demand. Kids line up for grandmother time," she said, humor dancing in her eyes.

He knew that was for his benefit, a reminder of his cross-examination of her about who watched his son while she worked. "Are you ever going to let me forget I was wrong?"

"Probably not."

"Good to know." He unbuttoned his coat and stretched his arm along the back of the booth, wishing he was touching the soft bare skin of her shoulder instead of leather.

Kate ran a finger over the red rose the maître d' had given her before showing them to their table in the back room by the brick wall. Joe had heard that subdued lighting was a girl's best friend, but Kate looked as sexy and beautiful in bright sunlight as she did by the glow of candles.

"The rose is a lovely touch," she said.

"I'm glad you like it."

He'd picked this place from an ad offering Gourmet Dining in a Romantic Atmosphere. Truth in advertising. Big time. He remembered Kate's surprise and pleasure over the single bud. Then, at their table, the waiter had produced a vase with water to keep it fresh through dinner before he'd wrap it up to take home.

Joe realized that if he'd known a single red rose would make her smile as if she'd been given the key to her own palace, he'd have given her a dozen when he picked her up. The only problem with looking at her looking like that was it made him want things he shouldn't want. Things like him, her, a bed and twisted sheets.

She unfolded the linen napkin in the basket and pulled out a slice of crusty French bread, then daintily dabbed butter on it before taking a bite. She stopped chewing for a moment, then said, "Hear that?"

"What?" He glanced around, straining to hear what she did. There was a low hum of voices and glass clinking.

"It's quiet." She met his gaze. "Doesn't it feel weird not to hear baby chatter? Or to have to jump up to change a diaper? Or funnel finger foods with one hand and hold your own fork with the other?"

"Now that you mention it…" He finished off his own bread.

A woman dressed in a white pleated shirt, black pants and a cummerbund appeared with a silver tool to scrape and catch the crumbs that had collected on the white linen tablecloth.

One corner of Joe's mouth lifted as he looked at Kate. "Do you suppose there's a gizmo like that for babies wearing teething biscuit from head to toe?"

"If that baby store doesn't have one, it doesn't exist."

"Yeah," he said, remembering the warehouse-sized store with aisle after aisle of infant and toddler equipment. He was pretty sure most of it hadn't been around when he was a kid. "In the olden days, how do you suppose new parents survived without all that stuff?"

Kate feigned a look of horror. "It's too awful to think about."

"Kind of gives you a new respect for the last generation, doesn't it?"

She nodded. "And speaking of that— I think I'll give Marilyn a call. Just to make sure everything is okay."

She pulled out her cell and hit speed dial. "Hi. It's Kate." She listened, then smiled. "Good." Staring at nothing she concentrated on the other end of the conversation. "Are you sure?" Nodding, she said, "Okay. It's wonderful. Thank you so much."

When she'd folded her phone and put it back in her purse, she looked at him. "Everything is fine. J.T. is sound asleep in the crib, down for the night. She says he's fine, relax and enjoy our evening out. We shouldn't worry about him, just plan on leaving him with her and not disturbing his sleep. She loves having him and her granddaughter wants to see him in the morning."

"Are you okay with that?" he asked.

"Are you?"

"You checked her out. She's got references."

She smiled. "Are you ever going to let me forget that?"

"Probably not." He turned his glass in a circle. "I found out for myself that you're a good judge of character. She's not just good with him. She loves him as if he's part of her family."

There was a relieved look on her face. "I'm glad you agree."

"We have consensus. J.T. is fine and we should relax."

"What if he wakes up and—"

He held up a finger. "So much for relaxed. I don't think you can get through the rest of dinner without talking about our son."

Her eyes narrowed. "I'm sensing a challenge."

"If you want to make it interesting, we can call it a bet. Whoever slips first has to pay up."

"You really don't think I can do it."

He shook his head. "I know you can't."

"Okay. You're on."

They clinked glasses to seal the deal, then she finished off the champagne in hers. Immediately a waiter unobtrusively refilled it from the bottle chilling in the bucket on a stand beside them.

"I love everything about this place," she said. "The service is amazing. You don't even have to ask. That's better than fast."

"Speaking of fast, you set a land/speed record getting ready tonight."

She tilted her head slightly and the brown silk of her hair brushed her bare shoulder. "When a handsome man shows up and says the baby is at the sitter, he's taking you to dinner so put on something nice, you don't waste time. You follow orders."

She hadn't just followed orders, he thought, drinking in the sight of her. The thin-strapped, low-cut black dress she wore was her salute. It was sexy as hell and all he could think about was how badly he wanted to take it off her. Finally her words sank in.

"You think I'm handsome?"

"Oh, please." A wry expression tugged at her full lips. "Every woman in this room is staring at you. I don't think I've ever seen you in a suit. Uniform, yes. And it's true what they say."

"What do they say?"

"There's something about a man in uniform that drives women nuts. But the civilian suit and tie is a really good look."

Joe didn't care about what other women thought. Only her.

When did that happen? Or had it always been that way and he'd refused to acknowledge it?

This was just supposed to be about doing something nice as a consolation prize, because he hadn't been there when she'd needed him. But was it more than a simple gesture of diplomacy?

A tuxedo-clad waiter took their orders—both filet mignon medium-rare. Then they made small talk, both making an effort to not lose the bet. Now he realized the folly of it. Their son was a neutral topic of conversation which he needed to keep his mind off how the sight of her made his hands shake. And, for the love of God, how could the place be air-conditioned until icicles formed yet he was hot as the Afghanistan desert in July?

Then he realized why. He'd voluntarily sent himself to hell.

He'd picked a romantic place. He was the one who'd dared her to put aside the safe topic of their son, which meant the conversation would turn personal. But he could still salvage the op. In spite of the dim light and hushed atmosphere, it was still very public and therefore safe.

Then he remembered that *public* hadn't stopped him before. It doesn't get more public than Mercy Medical Center. He'd already lost control once and kissed her at the hospital. Just like that—the taste of her, breathing in the scent of her skin, feeling her breasts pressed against his chest—all of it was right there in his mind. The sensations were two parts heaven, one part hell. And he was feeling the heat.

Chapter Eight

Kate felt the warmth of Joe's hand at the small of her back as he walked her to her door. Heat and awareness crackled through her at his slightest touch, and she was determined to ignore the sensations. His surprise dinner had been wonderful. But it was nothing more than a terrifically sweet gesture and she couldn't afford to believe otherwise. If she did, it would be déjà vu, and she was determined not to make the same mistake.

Finally they were at her door and the weird thing was she wasn't aware of getting there. All she knew was how profoundly cold and alone she felt when he removed his hand.

He unlocked her door and opened it, then followed her inside. Looking around, he said, "Everything looks okay."

"Just like I left it. Except it feels empty without J.T. here—" She stopped. "Oops. Did I just lose the bet?"

He laughed. "Lady, you talked about the baby ten seconds after we made that bet."

"Did not."

"The time frame might be accelerated, but the result is the same. You caved first."

"Okay." There was no point in arguing. She made an *L* with her thumb and index finger and rested it on her forehead. "Loser."

"So pay up."

She thought for a moment, then looked at him, all sexy with his jacket suspended by one finger over his shoulder, his tie loose at the neck with one button undone, wrinkles creasing the abdomen of his formerly crisp white shirt. The sight of him all masculine and rumpled gave her ideas. If his hand had felt that good, being in his arms would be like eating calorie-free chocolate.

"I don't remember setting the stakes for that bet," she said. "What do I owe you?"

His eyes grew intense just before he tossed his jacket on the end of her sofa and drew her tight against the length of him. She felt the ridge of his desire pressing into her and suddenly couldn't breathe. Was it the evidence of him wanting her, or was it being held so tightly in his arms? Or both?

"I can't say this is what you owe me because we didn't agree up front—" he lowered his mouth to within a whisper of hers "—but this is what I want."

Then he went all the way and captured her lips. It wasn't a sweet good-night kiss. This was an all-out assault on her senses. This was the aggressive warrior concentrating all of his considerable skill and training on victory. And he was good. With one arm around her waist, and the other threaded through her hair, exerting gentle pressure on the back of her head to make the contact more secure, he was winning the battle. But she was making it easy for him.

Her lips parted slightly and his tongue swept inside, establishing dominance, control and authority. His hand brushed up and down her back, generating sparks and heat. The sound of his labored breathing was harsh and extraordinarily wonderful.

If she was being honest, unlike the dinner, this wasn't a surprise. From the moment she first saw him dressed like a GQ model showing off corporate battle gear, sexual undercurrents had been flowing between them. It was a riptide of passion that she couldn't seem to break free of. And standing here in his arms she saw things more clearly than she had in a long time.

She didn't want to break free. She wanted him. Being in his arms was like coming home after a long, painful absence. The memories flashed through her mind like a sensual kaleidoscope. Gentle kisses, soft touches, whispered endearments. It was weak, stupid and foolish, but she wanted him—she wanted to feel again what he'd made her feel before. She was aware that her reasons for keeping him at arm's length were vital for her survival, but right at this moment, not one of them could keep her from the pleasure she knew was in his embrace.

Damn the torpedoes, full speed ahead. Let the shrapnel fall where it may.

Joe broke the contact and stared, his gaze raking over her face. He blew out a deep breath, then said, "I guess it's not top secret that I want you."

"I figured it out," she said, her own voice hoarse.

"And?" His eyes were probing and intense.

"I figure I want you, too."

"Are you sure?"

"Very." She couldn't look away, mesmerized and hypnotized by the tension clinging to the angles of his jaw, the curve of his mouth. She held her breath, waiting for the sensual assault that she craved more than her next breath. But he didn't move. "Joe?"

He ran his fingers through his hair. "I hurt you, Kate. I had no right to think about being with you like this. But I did. When I was a prisoner, I thought about holding you, making love to you. I don't deserve you—"

She shushed him with a finger to his lips. "Tonight there's no spreadsheet of who owes what. It's just sex. We're two people with a history who need someone tonight. No strings. No harm, no foul."

He looked troubled. "I don't want to hurt you again. I don't want to let you down."

Kate pulled on his tie, worked the knot loose, then slid the silk from underneath his collar and let it fall. She met his gaze and willed him to know what she felt. "As long as you're honest about your feelings. As long as you talk to me, you can't hurt me."

"Fair enough."

"Do you want me?"

The look in his eyes was mesmerizing as he pulled her against him. "I never stopped wanting you."

She released another button on his shirt. "Then I think we've done enough talking."

"You'll get no argument from me."

She'd said there was no energy for love, but she didn't have to dig to find enthusiasm for this. Standing on tiptoe, she pressed her mouth to his. His lips…umm…she loved that they could be take-no-prisoners hard one minute, then soft and coaxing the next. He smelled of sandalwood and spice and something unique that was all his own. The essence burrowed inside her and lit a fire everywhere it touched.

On the outside, his hands cupped her face while he kissed her senseless, then rested on her shoulders and brushed away the thin straps of her dress. He trailed kisses from the bare flesh where her strap had been to an exquisitely sensitive spot just beneath her ear. A moan of pleasure escaped her throat, torn from a mother lode of need deep inside.

Caught in the heat coursing through her and the tingles skipping over her skin, she barely felt the zipper at the back of her dress lower before the material slid down to pool at her feet. She stood in front of him wearing nothing but her strapless black lace bra, matching panties and all the insecurities about her post-pregnancy body.

Joe sucked in a breath at the sight of her. "Sweet mercy. If I'd known what was under that dress, I'd have swallowed my tongue a long time ago."

"Is that good?"

"You seriously don't know how hot you are?" he asked incredulously.

"I had a baby. I—" She shook her head.

His heated gaze and devil-may-care grin spoke volumes, but his words demolished her doubts. "The first time I saw you, I thought you were the most beautiful woman I'd ever seen. And now—" He reached out and curved his fingers over her hips, then stroked upward to cup her breasts through the lace. "No way in hell did I think you could possibly grow more beautiful, but, Katie, you shattered your own record."

"Right answer," she whispered, sucking in a breath when he brushed his thumbs over her nipples and brought them to attention. "I think we should take this conversation into the bedroom."

"Yes, ma'am."

She took his hand and led him down the hall, the light from the living room illuminating the way. The switch on the wall turned on a crystal lamp by the bed. Without hesitation, she pulled down the rose-patterned quilt, revealing the pink sheets underneath. Then she faced Joe and met his intense gaze as she started slowly opening the rest of the buttons on his shirt—one by one. When she finished, she pushed the material from his shoulders and he shrugged it off, tossed it carelessly aside.

She pressed her palms to his chest, loving the masculine dusting of hair. She slid her hands down to his flat abdomen and gloried in her power when his muscles quivered and his breathing quickened. His body had changed, too. He was leaner yet more muscular. Smooth, yet scarred where she didn't remember scars. When she reached out to touch one scar by his ribs, he caught her hand, shadows in his eyes. He brought her fingers to his lips, then drew each one into his mouth, sucking deeply before moving to the next.

After that, she couldn't think about anything but the knot of need expanding inside her. She backed up to the bed, pulling him with her before she sat, then slid over to make room for him. He kicked off his shoes, unbuckled his belt and slid off his slacks and boxers. Then he grabbed his wallet from the back pocket and pulled something out.

She stared at the square packet. "You brought a condom?"

"I'm an optimist. And a marine is always prepared."

If she'd had any doubts that he wanted her, that silenced them. "So you thought I'd be that easy?"

"You're anything *but* easy. I hoped," he said, his eyes filled with need and greed and tenderness.

Semper fi and thank goodness was all she could think before he took her in his arms and got down to business. His kisses were deep, drugging, determined, until her flesh was hot and liquid heat poured through her. With fortitude and an abundance of fine motor skills he swept her black panties off. Then he moved lower, kissed her right breast and nibbled his way down her stomach until she was quivering with desire. He cupped her bare hip in one big hand just before curving his fingers over her femininity and sliding one inside.

He stroked in and out, delving deep as he found the most extraordinarily sensitive spots. He was relentless and single-minded in his determination to give her pleasure. Her breath caught in her throat at the craving to have *him* inside her. How she'd missed him, missed this. It had been so long….

"I need you, Joe," she said, surprised at the hoarse longing in her voice.

He met her gaze, his expression intense, dark and bent on total possession as he reached for the condom. Bless those fine motor skills, she thought when he had the package open and the condom on in seconds. Then he levered himself over her, used his knee to spread her legs wider and with one stroke buried himself deep inside. The emptiness she'd carried for so long disappeared.

He moved in and out, friction building pleasure with each thrust. Arms around him, she dug her fingers into his back as with long, sweet strokes and lavish lazy glides he increased the tension inside her, building it higher and higher until she couldn't hold back. A burst of basic, electric sensation ripped from deep inside her and spread outward as a million bright lights exploded behind her eyes.

Moments later he tensed and bowed his head. With two deep thrusts he groaned out his own release, then rested his cheek to hers and sighed the deepest, most satisfied sigh she'd ever heard. After a quick kiss, he rolled away and disappeared into the bathroom. He was back in what seemed like moments. With one arm he gathered her close.

That was the last thing she remembered before a deep, gut-wrenching cry awakened her. She'd been so soundly asleep, it took several moments to recall what had happened and why Joe was in her bed. He mumbled and thrashed beside her, shouted something she couldn't understand. Obviously he was dreaming. Only what he was having was more like a nightmare.

She touched his bare shoulder, feeling the slick sweat. "Joe?"

He sat up instantly, surprising her. Breathing hard, he looked around, then down at her, his eyes anxious. "Kate?"

"Yeah. It's okay." She put her hand on his arm but he yanked it away. "Everything's okay."

He ran his fingers through his hair, then scrubbed his palms over his face. "I—I'm sorry," he said, throwing back the sheet.

He picked up his pants and slid them on, then walked out. Alarmed by his behavior, she grabbed a cotton robe and followed him into the living room where he was shrugging into his shirt.

"You're leaving?" she asked.

"I have to go." His voice was clipped, angry.

"You're welcome to stay. It's late. In the morning you can—"

"No." He walked to the door and opened it. "Trust me, it's for the best."

That's what he'd said the last time he'd left her. Now she knew what those words really meant and how much they hurt. And she hated herself for hurting again. She was the one who'd said it was just sex, which she'd sincerely believed at that moment. But being with him had been every bit as earth-shaking as she'd remembered. More, even. He'd taken her to a place they'd never been before, where life is astonishingly precious because she'd given birth and he'd faced death. The soul-shattering experience of being with Joe had made a lie of the words *no strings attached*.

Now she had to assess the damage and minimize it if possible.

It had been pathetically easy for him to charm his way back into her bed. Which made her all the more desperate to keep him from charming his way back into her heart.

Joe left the parking lot and walked through Kate's complex on his way to her apartment. She'd invited him to dinner tonight, before…Well, before he'd totally screwed everything up.

Why was it that when there was danger of losing something, you had a clear and unobstructed view of how profoundly important that something was? His life had changed in ways he'd never dreamed of since he'd come back. He'd gotten to know his son. Until J.T. he hadn't known it was possible to love so deeply.

And Kate?

That was complicated and he'd made it even worse. She'd had doubts about him in the beginning and he couldn't blame her. But he'd managed to gain her trust. Until last night. Sleeping with her had been heaven on earth. It had also turned into his worst nightmare. Literally. He'd been determined to keep his darkness away from her and had screwed up royally. But it wouldn't happen again because he didn't intend to touch her again. If he was a better man, he'd keep his distance. Since he was on his way to her apartment, clearly he wasn't a better man.

He both dreaded and longed to see her now. It had been a hell of a day after a sleepless night. Equipment and personnel problems had kept him grounded and scrambling at work. He hadn't been this bone-tired since his escape from the Taliban had kept him running and hiding until he'd finally come across a Marine Corps patrol in the foothills.

Memories of war, the terrible things he'd seen and done, were never as far from the surface as he'd like. The nightmare Kate had awakened him from was evidence of that. He'd handled the whole thing like a jerk, but all he could think about was keeping what happened over there from touching her and J.T. He'd hurt her enough already and only wanted to make her smile.

Just before he left her last night she hadn't been smiling. Hurt and confusion were in her eyes and he'd put them there. Like the lamebrain he was, he'd only said it was for the best. Did she still believe he was a good man?

He shook his head. If he was, he'd cut his losses and stay

out of her life. That way he couldn't hurt her again. But he was a father now and he had a responsibility to his boy. It was selfish and stupid, but he knew from experience with his own father that even a bad one was better than none at all. As ticked off as Kate probably was at him, he had a feeling even she would agree.

He knocked on the door, then shifted nervously as he waited. It was almost as bad as the first time, when he'd just returned from overseas. A shadow passed the window seconds before the door opened.

"Hi," he said, "is it—"

"I'm so glad you're here." She opened the door wider for him to step inside.

He did before she could change her mind. "You are?"

"I was going to have dinner ready. Stir-fry shrimp," she said. "But J.T. got fussy. What else is new at dinnertime? And I decided to give him a bath. He's on the floor in the bedroom. On a blanket."

"Not any more," he said pointing. The baby had crawled after her and was now grinning at Joe. "Hi, buddy."

Kate groaned. "It's a blessing and curse. I didn't truly appreciate the days when I put him down and he'd be in exactly the same spot when I came back."

"You do realize he's naked?"

J.T. had crawled over and was now pulling himself up by grabbing onto Joe's jeans. He bent and wrapped his fingers gently around the boy's upper arm for support.

Kate gave him a wry look. "By definition *bath* means washing without clothes. And that's why I'm glad you're here. He could go radioactive any second and it would be better if he wasn't in the living room."

"I see your point. You're the unit leader. What are my orders?"

"Could you start dinner?" She picked up the baby and his bare rump rested on her forearm. It was a new slant on courage. "There's a bag of frozen vegetables in the freezer. Directions are on it. When they're cooked, add the shrimp that's in the bowl. Teriyaki and soy sauce are already on the counter."

He saluted. "Understood. Roger that."

"Oh, please." She grinned before turning her back and heading down the hall.

He heard the water go on in the bathroom and figured Operation Clean Sweep was in progress. More important, Kate was glad he was there. Grinning, he walked into the kitchen and found all the ingredients as reported. Just like that, all was right with his world.

The frying pan was in the cupboard and he put olive oil and vegetables in to cook. A few minutes later Kate walked in with J.T. swaddled in a towel, his hair wet.

"Can you make some rice, too?" she asked. "There's a box in the pantry. It's the kind in a bag that you boil for ten minutes."

"No problem."

The expression on her face made him feel as if he'd done something truly heroic, but when she smiled, he felt the power of it clear inside, in a place so dark he'd thought nothing could light it up. He'd been wrong.

Whistling, he started the rice cooking and was just about to add the shrimp to the vegetables when there was a knock on the door. Since there was a steady stream of mother/son chatter from the bedroom, Joe figured she hadn't heard.

He opened the door and his gut tightened when he recognized his brother. "What the hell are you doing here, Preston?"

"Joe." The wrinkled blue dress shirt, tie and navy slacks were a clear indication that he'd come from the office. "What a nice surprise."

"That makes one of us." He braced his feet wide apart and stood in the doorway. No one, especially his brother, was getting past him. "I repeat, what the hell are you doing here?"

"I'm here to see my nephew." He folded his arms over his chest.

"Why?"

"Kate invited me."

The knot in his gut tightened and his fingers curled into fists. "You're lying."

"Despite what you think, little brother, I don't lie."

Joe narrowed his gaze. "We both know that's garbage."

"She came to see me on a quest to help you."

"I don't need your kind of help," he ground out. Kate had never said a word about seeing his brother, and instantly the light inside him sputtered out. "Stay away from Kate and my son."

"That boy is my family," Preston said, the muscle in his jaw jerking.

"Is that your excuse for everything? You think because you're the oldest it entitles you to what I've got? Like eminent domain?" Joe took a step forward. "This isn't like the last time, big brother. You're not taking what's mine. Not this time. Not ever again."

He stepped back and slammed the door. But when he turned, Kate was standing behind him and the shock on her face told him she'd heard everything.

Chapter Nine

"Joe?"

Kate stared at the man who both turned her on and fascinated her in equal parts. But this was a side of him she'd never seen, a fierceness that he kept tightly under control. He clenched his jaw so tightly the jagged scar stood out against his tanned skin.

"Where's J.T.?" he asked.

"He's in the crib, playing with his toys. I heard the door and came out to see who was here." And she'd gotten more than she bargained for. "Do you want to tell me what that was all about?"

"No."

"I wasn't really asking," she said.

"Good, because I'm not really in the mood to talk about it."

She folded her arms over her chest and planted her bare feet wide apart as she squared off right in front of him. He was a warrior, but she was prepared to take him on this time.

She lifted her chin and met his gaze. "Get in the mood.

You just threw an invited guest out of my home and I'd like to know why."

"You *did* ask him here?" Instead of lessening, his intensity cranked up, fueled by shock.

"Yes. He's J.T.'s uncle."

"When?"

"All the time. He's a Morgan."

The muscle in his jaw jerked. "That's not what I meant and you know it."

She did and stalling wouldn't help. "I went to see him at his office."

In Joe's blue eyes, fire turned to ice. "Why?"

"Clearly you're angry with your brother. Yet you manage to run a business together without having any kind of personal relationship. I wanted to know what's going on between you two."

"Why?" he asked again, his voice lower, deeper, deceptively calm and controlled.

"I could say that it's all about J.T., but that would only be part of the truth. The rest of it is that I'm damn curious and I care about you. This thing going on between you and Preston is eating you up and the only way to stop that is to get it out in the open."

"You're an emergency room nurse, right? Since when did you start working the psych section?"

"Wow. Sarcasm." His tone was cutting and nicked her feelings, but she shook it off. When a warrior felt cornered he came out swinging. She held her ground, fighting for him, because he was her son's father. Anything beyond a DNA connection she didn't want to think about.

"You can do better than that, Joe. Give me your best shot, because I'm not letting you off the hook until you tell me what's bugging you."

"You really want to know?" He took a step forward until

their bodies were barely brushing and the fire was back in his eyes. "It ticks me off that you went to see him at all. I hate that you were anywhere near that bastard."

"Let me remind you that he's the reason you know about J.T." She straightened to her full height which wasn't much help since he towered over her. She raised her chin higher and looked him in the eye. "If not for your brother I wouldn't have known where to send that letter to let you know you were going to be a father. Instead of thanking him, you threw him out. I'm going to give you the benefit of the doubt and assume you had a good reason. But I really want to know what it is."

The anger and resentment built up as he ran his fingers through his hair. "Okay. I'll tell you why, but remember you asked for it. He's a backstabbing son of a bitch. My brother, my *family*," he said, irony underlining the word, "slept with my wife while I was overseas."

She'd asked for it and she got it in spades. That had never occurred to her. "Oh, Joe—are you sure? How do you know?"

"She told me. I was barely off the plane before she confessed and said she'd filed for divorce." He turned away, as if he couldn't tolerate the sympathy in her eyes. "I confronted my brother and he didn't deny it."

"I don't know what to say. Except he's your family and you need to talk about it, Joe. People make mistakes—"

He whirled around to face her, his eyes blazing. "You can say that again. And a lot of them were mine. My dad warned me that she was only after money, but I wouldn't listen. Before I left for the Middle East, she told me she'd wait and I believed her." Bitterness rolled off him in waves. "I was hardly wheels-up before she jumped in the sack with my brother. My guess is that she was hedging her bets on the Morgan bucks and he was only too happy to oblige."

"I'm sorry you had to go through that."

Kate knew the words were pathetically inadequate to express the depth of her feelings, but she didn't know what else to say. And she didn't know what to make of his brother's involvement. Both times she'd seen Preston Morgan, he had seemed like an honorable man, but how could he be?

"Don't waste pity on me," he said. "It's ancient history. I'm over it."

"Oh?" She slid her hands into the pockets of her shorts. "I'd be more inclined to believe that if you weren't so upset that I went to see him. And I don't really understand your reaction."

"You really don't get it?" His eyes flashed. "I can't stand the thought of him coming on to you. The idea of him with his hands all over you."

Was it really his brother he was worried about? Or was it her? That she might have been with his brother behind his back? That he could be betrayed again? He'd failed in his father's eyes and in his own. He didn't want to trust another woman and make another mistake. It had to be that, because jealousy required a deeper, personal connection.

She rested her palm on the tense muscles in his forearm. "I can take care of myself."

He stared at her for several moments before finally covering her hand with his own. "Don't you see? I don't want you in a situation where you have to."

As she studied his hard jaw and the shadow of betrayal in his eyes, his words echoed through her mind. *She said she'd wait.* And suddenly Kate understood why he'd broken things off with her so abruptly before he'd deployed.

He couldn't ask her to wait for him because he was afraid she wouldn't.

The deceit and disloyalty had been a double whammy—his

wife and his brother. Why should he believe he could trust someone he'd known for only a short time? No matter that she was completely gone over him. He wouldn't believe that.

Kate didn't know what to do and finally took a step forward and wrapped her arms around his waist, rested her cheek on his chest. He stood rigid for several moments and then folded her against him as he let out a shuddering sigh.

So there was one secret out in the open. The haunted expression in his eyes when she'd opened the door to him earlier hinted at his nightmare and told her that there were still secrets he was determined to keep. And she wasn't sure that coaxing him to confide would be in her best interest.

He had good, solid, emotional reasons for actions that had hurt her deeply. Rationally, she finally forgave him for dumping her, the same way she'd forgiven him for ignoring her letter about being pregnant. She knew him better now; she knew how much deeper he could hurt her if she let her guard down.

If she ever forgave him with her heart, she would be in a world of hurt.

It was seven in the evening and still over a hundred degrees outside, but Joe would take the Vegas desert over Afghanistan any month of the year, including July. He walked from the guest parking and followed the curving sidewalk through Kate's complex. He didn't feel like a guest. It was more like coming home, he realized. And that was three parts weird and one part wonderful. He had a spacious house in one of the valley's most exclusive areas and her small apartment had turned into the staging area for his life.

Maybe not so weird, since Kate and J.T. had saved his life.

If not for the need to meet his son and see Kate again, he wasn't sure he'd have been able to do what he'd needed to do to get out of that hellhole. Now he owed it to them to leave all that darkness on the other side of the world, not let it touch their lives.

Mostly he was successful. Except the one time he'd let down his guard after falling asleep in her bed. Okay, twice—she'd dragged that crap with his brother out of him. When Kate made up her mind it was impossible to hold her off in an all-out assault.

And speaking of resisting… Every time he saw Kate, he found it harder to resist her. Maybe that wouldn't be so if he hadn't already slipped up and made love to her. As he jogged up the stairway to her apartment, he realized it wouldn't make any difference. He would always ache from wanting her. But he was determined to prove his father was wrong about him being a screwup and do the right thing. The right thing would be keeping his hands off her even if it killed him.

The thing was, he'd felt as though he was on probation with Kate. She'd made it clear she didn't trust him and he couldn't really blame her. Lately her attitude wasn't showing so much, even though he'd crossed the line into her bed. Over the last couple of weeks she'd never asked why he'd refused to stay the night. The truth was he couldn't risk another nightmare; he wanted to keep that darkness away from her.

Since then, it had been business as usual—sharing responsibility for J.T. and visiting the two of them whenever he wanted. Like tonight.

Suddenly eager to see Kate and his son, he knocked on her door and waited. And waited.

Unlike the first time, when he'd shown up unexpectedly, it never took her this long to answer, even if she was busy with the baby.

"Kate?" He knocked again, a little harder.

Uneasiness trickled through him. They'd talked last night and she knew he was coming by after work. Her car was in the lot.

Instinct had him trying to see in the window, but the blinds were closed. "Kate, open up."

When there was no response, he used the key she'd given him and unlocked the door. He pushed his sunglasses up to the top of his head. "Kate?"

"Joe—"

It took several moments for his eyes to adjust from the bright sunlight outside, then he saw her in the doorway to the hall. Dressed in a baggy white T-shirt and cutoff sweat shorts, her brown hair was tangled around her face and she was doubled over.

In seconds he was beside her. "What's wrong?"

"Pain in my stomach. Started during the night—"

He slid his arm around her waist and helped her sit on the sofa. "Where's J.T.?"

She slumped sideways. "I called Marilyn. She picked him up and took him home with her."

"You should have called me."

"Didn't want to bother you at work." She winced and folded her arms over her abdomen, then started to shiver.

He felt her forehead and frowned. "Do you have a ther-mometer?"

"Way ahead of you. It's a hundred and two—" Her face tensed and she groaned as she pulled her knees up, curling into fetal position.

"I'll get you something for the fever."

"Already did. A little while ago."

"Then it's not working."

"Could be my appendix. But probably not. I think it's a flu," she said. "You should go before you catch it."

"I'll take the risk."

She needed fluids. He left her and went into the kitchen, pulling a bottle of water from the refrigerator. After twisting off the cap, he squatted beside her then slid a hand beneath her head to help her drink.

"Drink a little," he urged.

She grimaced and shook her head. "Can't. Stomach's not feeling so good."

Joe studied her as worry knotted inside him. There was no color in her face and her full lips were dry. She wouldn't or couldn't get water down and her fever wasn't responding to over-the-counter medication. He was a chopper pilot, not a medic, but this was basic.

"I'm taking you to Mercy Medical," he said.

"No." She shook her head. "I'm just sick."

"News flash," he said, gently cupping her face in one hand as he brushed his thumb over her pale cheek. "They take care of sick people there."

"It's not serious."

She was arguing and that should have made him feel better. It would have if she was going toe-to-toe with him instead of curled in a ball. She was the strongest person he knew and seeing her like this ripped him up. Without another word, he lifted her into his arms.

"Joe— No—"

"I'll believe it's nothing when a doctor tells me."

"I'll feel like an idiot when they send me home with a diagnosis of the flu," she protested.

"Blame it on me. I can take it. I've got broad shoulders."

She grabbed on to his neck then rested her head on her arm as if it was too heavy to hold up. "Nice shoulder. Strong. Good to lean on."

And that's when he really started to worry, because if there wasn't something seriously wrong, she would never have admitted that.

* * *

Joe paced the E.R. waiting room where they'd told him to sit tight while the doctor examined Kate. He wasn't sure how long it had been, but it seemed like forever. Surely they must know something by now. He'd made up his mind to charge through the double doors and find her when he turned and nearly collided with a small redhead in blue scrubs.

"Mr. Morgan?"

"Yes. It's Joe. Kate introduced us. You're Sandy Richardson."

"That's right. Good memory."

"How is she?" he asked.

"She wants to see you. Come with me."

He followed her through the doors and down the hall, then Sandy pushed aside a privacy curtain. "Here he is."

Kate was in the bed. She was wearing a hospital gown and had a white cotton blanket over her legs. There was an IV in her arm. Her mouth curved in a small smile when she saw him. "Hi."

"Hey."

"Thanks for getting him," Kate said weakly.

Sandy nodded, then yanked on the curtain to close it. "I'll be back in a couple of minutes."

Joe pulled a chair over and sat down beside her. Traces of pain still lingered in her eyes. "How do you feel?"

"Like roadkill."

"Is it the flu?" Please God she'd been right about that.

She shook her head as her forehead puckered with worry. "That's why I asked Sandy to get you. I hoped I was wrong. But it is my appendix. They're going to take it out."

"You need surgery?"

"As soon as they can get me into the O.R.," she confirmed.

His chest tightened with something close to panic. He'd been under fire and taken prisoner by terrorists. He'd faced the unknown, planned his escape, pulled it off then eluded jihadist thugs who wanted nothing more than to put a slug in his head. But he'd never experienced the kind of fear he felt now.

She must have seen because she put her hand on his. Her fingers were like ice. "It's not serious—"

"Surgery isn't serious?"

"Of course. It's a concern any time there's general anesthesia involved. But I'm young and in good health. No reason to borrow trouble. It's a simple procedure." Her words were a little slurred and her voice raspy. She'd probably gotten something for the pain. "I left voice mail on my mom's cell. Maybe she can come in from Pahrump and help with J.T. It's only an hour away. I'll keep trying her—"

"Not necessary."

"It is. Marilyn didn't plan—"

"Already taken care of. She agreed to keep him until I can pick him up. She said to tell you to relax and feel better."

"You called her?"

"Yeah. You were a little busy."

She caught her top lip between her teeth. "I'm sorry you got stuck with this."

Irritation momentarily squeezed out the fear. "For crying out loud, Kate. He's my son, too. It's not like you're asking for a kidney. I'll handle it. Just let go. You don't have to be strong all the time."

She nodded even as her eyes were drifting shut.

He wanted so badly to hold her, but that was out of the question, so he bent his head and touched his lips to her fingers. "Just be okay."

"This is my turf," she said drowsily. "They'll take good care of me."

"If not, they'll answer to me."

The privacy curtain was pushed aside and Sandy stood there. "They're going to take you to the O.R. now."

Kate smiled at him. "Man the battle stations."

"Give 'em hell," he said.

When two guys in blue scrubs stepped up and wheeled her out, he felt as though his world had imploded.

"Will she really be okay?" he asked.

Sandy glanced over her shoulder, then met his gaze, green eyes cool and assessing. "She's healthy. You brought her in right away. Fortunately Mitch Tenney was on. Appendicitis can be tricky to diagnose, but he got it in five minutes. The sooner they get it out, the better. The procedure's not complicated unless her appendix ruptures. If not, it shouldn't take long. There's a surgery waiting room upstairs. That is if you're staying."

"Of course I'm staying."

She shrugged. "Okay."

He had one nerve left and this pint-sized pessimist had just stomped on it. "What's your problem?"

"I'm looking at him." She folded her arms over her chest and glared.

"I haven't known you long enough for us to have an issue."

"Kate's my friend," she said.

"Okay." He stared at her. "And your point?"

"She's having an invasive procedure that will require some recovery time. That's not going to be easy with an active baby."

"I'll make it easy for her."

"So you'll still be around when she's ready to go home?"

"That's my plan." Anger coursed through him and it was a welcome relief from the fear. "I'm taking care of my son and his mother. Not that it's any of your concern. Where do you get off—"

"See, that's the thing. I didn't get off. You did." She pointed accusingly at him. "It's my concern because after you took off I was there to listen when she poured her heart out. What was left of her heart after you got finished with it."

She gave him one last glare, then turned on her heel and walked away.

Joe felt as if she'd punched him in the gut. He knew Kate didn't trust him. He knew she had reason, but he couldn't have asked her to wait. He couldn't go through that again. Now he understood that she didn't believe anyone stuck around, and he'd reinforced that belief by walking out on her.

Well, he was back now. To stay.

Not far from where he was standing, she'd told him he was a good man. He didn't believe it now any more than he had then. He hadn't been enough for his wife. He hadn't been able to save his buddy in Afghanistan. And he still doubted he could keep the bad stuff buried and be good enough for Kate and his son, but he was selfish enough not to walk away.

Kate would need help when she got out of the hospital. He would keep showing up… No. Just showing up wasn't good enough. He could do better than that. She needed him really to be there for her. And the baby.

It would be harder to keep his distance emotionally, but he'd survived brutal captivity by compartmentalizing his emotions. That's what he would have to do now.

He wasn't just going to show up, he was moving in with her.

Chapter Ten

"Hi, Mom." Kate sucked in a breath at the pain that ground through her midsection when she reached for the phone.

On her bed, she leaned back against the plush pillows encased in pink percale and said good-bye to her lovely nap. Afternoon sunlight glowed through the sheers at her windows and spread across her room with its oak dresser and nightstands.

"How are you feeling, Katie?"

"Don't worry. I'm fine."

"I just got your message. I'm so sorry I wasn't here. Bill and I went away. I turned off my cell phone."

"Bill?" She should have known better than even to ask.

"Yeah. I'm sure I mentioned him before. He's one of my regulars at the coffee shop—"

Kate tuned out the rest when Joe walked into the bedroom and she pointed to the phone and mouthed, *Mom*.

"You okay?" he said softly.

She nodded, and he set the glass of juice on the nightstand beside the crystal lamp and left. The sight of his broad back in a snug navy-blue T-shirt made her want to sigh, and that had nothing to do with discomfort from her surgery.

"Kate? Are you there?"

Instantly she was pulled from the brink of fantasyland and back into reality. "Yeah, Mom. I'm glad you and Bill clicked."

"He's really wonderful, sweetie." Candy's euphoric sigh was audible. "I just feel so bad that I wasn't there when you needed me. I didn't even come to the hospital to visit."

"It's okay. Joe took me to the E.R. I was in and out so fast it would hardly have been worth the trip."

It was a blur of pain, medication and exhaustion. The surgery was textbook. No complications. About thirty-six hours after the attack she was minus one appendix and home recovering. Thanks to Joe.

"Well, I'm available now," Candy assured her. "Say the word. I can be there in an hour."

"It's not necessary. I'm doing fine."

"What about J.T.? After even a minor surgery I wouldn't think you should pick him up."

"You're right. The doctor said I should avoid heavy lifting."

"I could come and take care of him."

"It's okay, Mom. Joe's helping out. He's here now."

"Oh." After a pregnant pause, she said, "It's about four o'clock. I could be there by dinnertime and stay tonight. When he goes home. So you can relax."

Relax was a relative term and that was no pun at her mother's expense. Joe had brought her home from the hospital and announced he was staying. Overnight. On the couch. There was a part of her that hadn't relaxed since.

"He's not going home. He slept on my sofa last night."

After several moments of silence Candy said, "Good. I'm glad you have help."

"Me, too."

"Is there anything else you want to tell me?"

Kate could think of a million things but knew her mother was referring to personal stuff with Joe. Her instinct was to say there was nothing, but knew that would instigate a marathon interrogation. So she threw a bone.

"He insisted on staying." She'd tried to talk him out of it, but was at a disadvantage, what with the post-surgery weakness. He'd picked her up and set her in the bed very gently. Then he'd reminded her he was a marine and could handle any situation, including a stubborn woman. Until a doctor declared her fit for duty, she was on the inactive list and he was on patrol to make sure she followed orders. "J.T. loves having him here."

"What about you?" Candy asked.

"It's fine."

Oh, brother. That didn't even scratch the surface of her feelings but no way was she going there. Not with her mother. Not with Joe just in the other room.

"Look, Mom, I—"

"Hold on, sweetie. I've got another call."

Kate opened her mouth to say she'd just hang up, but heard the click and knew she was on hold. She carefully shifted to her left hip as she waited. Then there was another click that told her Candy was back.

"Hi, baby. I have to go. My guy's on the other line."

"Okay. Thanks for calling, Mom. Good luck with Bill."

"I don't need luck. It's all just good. Bye, baby. Take care of yourself. Love you."

Kate sighed and replaced the phone in the cradle beside the bed. She took the glass and sipped orange juice through the straw. Then she heard a wail from across the hall. It was the touchy time after J.T.'s nap and before dinner. He could be crabby, tired, hungry or just teething. Joe had walked the floor with him last night when he woke up. What would she have done if he hadn't been there? She wasn't sure when she could even pick him up without risk.

"Hey, marine?" she called. "Is J.T. okay?"

The next moment Joe appeared in the doorway, holding the baby. As soon as J.T saw her he held out his chubby arms and started squirming as he chanted, "Unh, unh."

"In my expert opinion," Joe said, "he wants a little mom time."

"And I need a little baby-boy time," she said, holding out her arms.

"How's your pain level?" he asked.

Before leaving the hospital they'd explained how to quantify her discomfort. As a nurse she'd been aware, but it was all different on this side of the medical fence.

She thought about the dull ache. "It's not that bad. I just really need to hold him."

"Are you sure?"

"Yeah. It hurts me more that he's feeling something's not right, but he doesn't understand. I need to reassure him."

"Okay." Joe carried him to the side of the bed and set him on her lap, then stood guard beside them.

"Hey, sweetheart. Mommy's here," she crooned when J.T. curled into her and rested his cheek on her chest.

It was too much to hope that an active boy would stay like that for very long. Almost instantly, he lifted his head and looked around, spotting the glass and straw beside them. He reached out unsuccessfully with plump fingers, then squirmed around, making her suck in a breath when he braced a knee inches from her incision.

Joe grabbed him up and when the boy cried out, he held him high over his head, managing to get a belly laugh from the child. She might be feeling as though someone had thrown her under a bus, but at least J.T. had his father. His strong, handsome, tender, heroic father had come along just in the nick of time.

Even before Joe took her to the E.R., Kate had suspected there was something really wrong with her. They said health-care professionals made the worst patients and she'd been no exception. But it was more about hoping whatever it was would just go away. She'd always managed on her own.

"That was a close call." Joe settled J.T. on his strong forearm and the child instantly held out his arms to her again.

"He doesn't know any better," she said, her heart aching because normally she loved having him close to her. There was no way to explain why he couldn't be.

"I know. But I'm not taking any chances that you'll get hurt."

"Just set him on the bed. You, too," she suggested. Her face went hot and it wasn't about fever. "That way you can grab him before he gets into trouble."

"The jostling won't make you uncomfortable?"

She was uncomfortable, but not because of surgery or the baby. Just having Joe this close made her uncomfortable in a very man/woman kind of way. Was he remembering as vividly as she that the last time they'd been in this room together, both of them were naked? "No. It won't make me uncomfortable."

"Okay." He walked around the bed and set the baby down, then stretched out on the other side of the queen-sized mattress.

J.T. crawled back and forth between them, pulled himself to a standing position using the headboard, wiggled to the end of the bed where he stared at the floor as if it was completely fascinating while his daddy kept him from serious head injury by holding on to his foot. All she had to do was watch. And enjoy. This was completely unfamiliar territory.

This feeling of complete and utter contentment made absolutely no sense. How could she hurt so much from the trauma her body had been through and be so happy at the same time?

J.T. crawled beneath the covers and lay on his back, looking up at her. "Ma?"

"Hey, baby boy." Kate brushed his curling dark hair off his forehead. "He's getting so big. Pretty soon he won't be a baby any more."

"Yeah."

"It will be nice when he's potty-trained and I can go out without a diaper bag. Of course that will mean public restrooms, which is a whole different level of scary."

Until this moment she'd never wondered how she would handle that. Let him go in the men's room alone? The thought made her cringe. Take him in the ladies' room? Not very masculine. But now his father was here to deal with the dynamics of all that. And she had no doubt he could. He was a marine. He'd rushed her to the hospital and made sure J.T. was in good hands. When he brought her home, he'd cooked, cared for the baby and fetched for her.

She looked at Joe. Blue eyes so intense, so vigilant as he guarded his son. Broad shoulders that had carried the responsibility since she'd been sick. What would she have done without him? The hardest thing about that question was that she feared it was emotional as opposed to logistical.

Then she looked at the baby who had plopped himself on his father's wide chest. Her eyes suddenly filled with tears. Unfortunately Joe chose that moment to look at her and it was too much to hope he wouldn't notice.

Instantly, he tensed. "Are you in pain?"

"No." Not physically anyway.

"What's wrong?"

She sniffled. "I guess I'm just tired."

"Do you always cry when you're tired?"

"If J.T. can do it, so can I." She rubbed a finger beneath her nose, completely mortified and trying to brazen it out. "Like mother, like son."

Without a word, Joe slid over and gently pulled her close, settling his strong arm around her while their son used his chest for a playground. She remembered him saying she didn't always have to be strong. But he was wrong. She'd always been able to do it by herself.

Except this time. What if Joe hadn't been here? That was a scary thought. But she had another that was worse. What if she let herself count on him completely? What if she let herself care and he walked out on her? She couldn't take that risk.

Kate waited for ten minutes after Joe and J.T. left for the grocery store before pulling out the bucket and mop to do a thorough cleaning on the kitchen floor. She glanced at the digital clock on the microwave over the stove and figured the list she'd given him would give her about an hour and a half. After a week of him not letting her lift a finger she was about to go out of her mind.

She quickly used her electric broom to suck up surface dirt, then filled the bucket with hot water and soap. It didn't take her long to do the rest, including the bathroom.

She smiled with satisfaction as she surveyed the results. "I could eat off that floor."

The knock on the door startled her. She wasn't expecting anyone and Joe wouldn't knock because he had a key. At least she hoped he hadn't forgotten it. Even if he had, he'd find another way in. No way would he give her an excuse to get up off the sofa. No way would he give her a pass to leave her bed unless basic bodily functions were involved. Washing the floor was mutiny in the ranks.

She walked over, peeked out the window and grinned. After turning the dead bolt, she opened the door. "Sandy! You're a sight for sore eyes."

Her friend gave her a hug. "The last time I saw you it wasn't your eyes that were sore. What's it been? A week?"

"I think so," Kate agreed.

Sandy gave her a once-over from head to toe. "You look good."

"Come on in." She shut the door, then saw the cleaning stuff still in the kitchen. "Let me get rid of that."

After stashing the mop in the closet, she bent to lift the full bucket. A dull ache in her right lower quadrant made her wince.

"I'll do that," Sandy said, reaching out for the handle. "I can't believe you did this. What's wrong with you? You're an R.N."

"Yeah. And you know what they say."

"Bad patient. You're irrefutable proof that it's true," her friend said, shaking her head as she dumped the water down the kitchen sink. After rinsing thoroughly, she stowed the bucket then glared at Kate. "A clean house is not more impor-tant than your health. I'm sure your doctor's advice was to take care of you and the baby. Everything else can wait. A little dirt won't kill you."

"See that's just it, Sandy." Kate leaned back against the counter. "I'm going stir-crazy. I haven't been able to do anything."

"You call fetching and carrying for that little guy nothing?"

"No. But the big guy is doing that."

Sandy looked confused. "What are you talking about?"

Suddenly tired, Kate said, "Can we sit?"

"Want me to piggyback you to the couch?"

"Not necessary." Kate gave her a wry look.

"I'll get us a cold drink."

While Kate settled herself in the living room, her friend put ice and water in two glasses and carried them over. She settled them on cardboard coasters imprinted with the marks of J.T.'s teeth.

"Put your feet up," Sandy advised, sitting far enough away to make room. She glanced around and her gaze settled on the hunter-green glider chair on the other side of the coffee table. "I don't remember that."

"It's new. Joe bought it." And he'd remembered green was her favorite color.

"I see." Her tone dripped disapproval.

Kate eased back against the throw pillows and sighed. "I hate to admit it, but that feels good. Did Joe send you to check up on me?"

"No." Sandy sipped her water and wrapped her hands around the glass. "I hadn't heard from you and was concerned. Your mom isn't close by and I was afraid you were on your own."

"No." Kate would have been except for Joe.

"I gather Joe's monitoring your recuperation. Is he the big guy fetching and carrying J.T.?"

Kate nodded. "He gets very macho and military when I disobey orders and try to do anything."

"How's that working for you?"

Way too well, Kate thought. "He's been great," she said cautiously.

"That's good."

"Yeah. He picked me up from the hospital and has been sleeping here ever since."

Kate brushed her hand over the material beside her, imagining the warmth from his body. His continued presence in her small space made her more grateful than was wise. It was probably a criteria for crazy that she was actually happy her appendix had been yanked out, giving her a chance to spend time with him.

Her abdomen knotted with something that had nothing to do with her surgery and everything to do with the man who'd invaded her life like a conquering hero. He hadn't made a single move on her since the night they'd made love, and, more than anything, she wanted him to kiss her like that again. Being in his arms would be good, too. She'd liked it there when he'd comforted her.

"What is it, Kate?" There was a disapproving note in Sandy's voice.

"I don't know what you mean."

"You've got that look on your face."

"What? Am I pale?" She put her hands to her cheeks. "I know I've been cooped up, but cut me some slack. I had surgery."

"It's not that post-surgery recuperation look." Sandy put her elbows on her knees and stared. "It's a symptom of reinfection from the romance virus. Joe is getting to you all over again. Although I have to give him a point or two for sticking around to help this time."

Kate wanted to blow off the statement, but that wasn't fair. Her friend had been there for her through major heart trauma. The least she could do was be honest.

"He had a good reason for dumping me before he left."

"Really? Care to share?"

"Besides me, you are the most skeptical woman on the planet," Kate said shaking her head. "Of course I'll share. He was married when he went overseas the first time. When he got back expecting a family reunion, he found out she'd cheated on him with his brother."

Sandy's green eyes widened in shock as she set her empty water glass on the coaster. "Holy cow—"

"No kidding." Kate tucked her hair behind her ear. "So when he got his orders to go back, he broke it off with me."

"But why? There are a hundred ways he could have handled it. No promises. Let's keep in touch. Letters. See what happens when I come back. Take your pick," she said throwing her hands up.

"It's easy to be rational now." Kate rested her hands in her lap. "I think he didn't want to have any expectations at all because he couldn't handle more disillusionment. Think about it, Sandy. He went away and lost his family. Why would he put any faith in a woman he barely knew?"

Sandy opened her mouth for a trademark snarky comeback, then shut it again. She blew out a long breath. "I got nothin'. Your point is well taken."

"I'm glad you get it."

Kate hated being the rational one. She really wished she could maintain her hostility level for the man who'd hurt her. She didn't want to put faith in him any more than he'd wanted to trust her.

"So what are you going to do about him?" Sandy asked.

"What do you mean?"

Sandy toyed with a loose strand of red hair from the ponytail on top of her head. "He's hanging around. He's your son's father." She shrugged. "What are you going to do about him?"

"Why do I have to do anything?"

"He asked you to marry him. Where does that stand?"

Good question. Kate had been so busy standing guard while Joe learned to be a father that she hadn't had time to think about it.

"I turned him down," she reminded her friend.

"How do you feel about that now?"

"For crying out loud, Sandy. Why do you always ask the hard questions?"

Green eyes brimmed with sympathy, friendship and affection. "Someone has to. It's what good friends do."

Kate folded her arms over her chest. "I don't know how I feel about turning him down. Relieved, maybe."

"Regret, maybe?"

"No way." Kate shook her head. "That proposal was just a knee-jerk reaction to finding out he was a father. Since then he's realized that we can parent together without being married."

"If he asked you now what would you say?"

"Again with the hard questions," Kate complained.

"You don't have to answer."

"Good. So how are things at the hospital?"

Sandy grinned at the awkward segue. "The same. Everyone is overworked, underpaid and stressed out. And Dr. Tenney is driving everyone nuts. The thing is, I have to admire him for telling it like it is."

Kate knew what she meant. "He says the politically incorrect things everyone else is thinking but won't say."

"Yeah." Sandy rested her elbows on her knees. "He's a brilliant E.R. doc but if he doesn't take a sensitivity pill, that abrasive streak is going to cost him. Possibly his job."

"I hope not. I'm glad he was on duty when Joe brought me in." Kate knew firsthand how good Mitch Tenney was. He'd diagnosed her "hot appendix" right away and expedited treatment when it was close to rupturing and pouring the poison through her. If that had happened, recuperation might have been far more complicated. "It would be a shame if the hospital loses him."

"Yeah. It would." Sandy stood up. "Now that I've seen with my own eyes that you're fine, I've got to go."

"You can't stay until Joe gets back with J.T.?"

"He won't want to see me," Sandy said.

"The baby loves you."

"I mean Joe." She pulled her car keys from her shorts pocket. "I kind of let him know that I thought he was a jerk. When he brought you in."

Kate sat up and swung her legs over the edge of the sofa. "What did you say?"

"I just wondered out loud if he'd be around when you were ready to go home."

So he'd stepped up out of a sense of duty? Challenge? Worse. He'd been guilted into the role of nursemaid. The small bubble of hope and happiness expanding inside her developed a slow leak.

"He's made everything really easy on me," Kate said. "And by the way, if you see him, don't rat me out about doing the kitchen floor."

Sandy laughed. "If you swear not to do it again until fully recovered."

"I promise." Kate made a cross over her heart.

The other woman walked to the door and opened it, then hesitated before turning back. "For the record, maybe I was wrong about Joe."

That was the last thing Kate wanted to hear. She needed ammunition to harden her resolve, not a free pass to fall in love.

Since getting sick, Kate had glimpsed her vulnerability in a way she never had before. In the past she'd counted on friends. After her medical crisis and living with Joe she knew there were places in her heart that good friends couldn't fill.

This time when he left her it would feel more empty than ever before.

Chapter Eleven

Joe left work early and picked J.T. up at Marilyn's. Kate had been right on about that woman. Every kid with parents who worked should have a Marilyn-type grandmother for backup when plan A went haywire.

With the little guy nestled in his arms and dozing on his shoulder, he unlocked the apartment door then walked in and glanced around. "Kate?" he said softly.

The doc had said it would take up to three weeks post-op until she could resume her normal schedule. She was one week post-op and still tired easily, often napping in the afternoon. He moved stealthily down the hall courtesy of Marine Corps Drill Sergeant Bates and thought it ironic that his military training could have civilian applications. In her bedroom, Kate was propped up on pillows and sound asleep with a book in her lap.

Her thick lashes rested against the smooth skin of her cheek and his fingers ached to trace the curve and cup it in his palm.

For just a moment, he let himself look his fill at her mouth while his body tightened with the need to kiss her, to make love to her again. For one week he'd slept just a few feet from where she was now and used every ounce of self-control he possessed not to slide in bed beside her and just take her in his arms. Feel her skin pressed to his.

Even if he dared to get that close, he wouldn't do more than hold her. He wouldn't hurt her—body or soul. But he wanted to touch her and love her. He longed for it, ached for it and fought it as he'd never fought before. And that's why he stayed put night after agonizing night and tried not to look at her too much during the day.

He'd learned early on he couldn't shut out the sweet smell of her skin, but being under the same roof was a different level of torture. With a shuddering sigh, he walked away from her and shut the hallway door so she wouldn't be disturbed. He set the diaper bag on the coffee table, trying to decide what to do with the little guy in his arms when there was a knock on the door. The baby stirred and turned his head, rubbing his face across Joe's shoulder. Weird how that small, trusting movement made his chest ache with tenderness.

He answered the door and found a woman there. She was in her late forties or early fifties and didn't look as though she was selling anything.

Joe gave her his don't-mess-with-me-I'm-a-marine look. "Whatever it is, this isn't a good time. The baby's asleep and I don't—"

"Are you Joe?"

"Yes." He didn't recognize her, but she might work at the hospital.

The woman standing there gave him a thorough once-over. "I'm Candy, Kate's mother."

He saw the resemblance now—same height, eyes, hair color. Looking at her solved the mystery of where Kate's dimples had come from, but this woman's face showed evidence of a hard life. He had no right to be glad Kate hadn't followed in her mother's footsteps, but that didn't make it any less true.

"Nice to meet you," he said. "Kate's sleeping, but—"

Candy held up her hand. "Don't wake her. I don't want her to be concerned. I was in the area for a doctor's appointment."

"Is something wrong?"

Her hazel eyes were shadowed even as she smiled and shook her head. "Not really, no. It was a checkup. How's Kate doing?"

"Good. Look, do you want to come in?" he asked.

"I don't want to intrude." Her face softened as she brushed a finger along the back of the baby's leg. "Although I don't get to see as much of my grandson as I'd like. I live over an hour away in Pahrump."

"Kate mentioned that." He stepped back.

Candy came inside and he closed the door. She looked longingly at the baby. "Would it be all right if I held him?"

"Sure." He angled his chin toward the glider he'd recently bought. It took the edge off walking the floor with a teething kid who couldn't sleep. "Sit there and I'll hand him over."

She set her purse on the floor and did as he suggested. When he put the child in her arms J.T. stirred and she moved the chair, gliding easily to settle him down again. "So Kate's recovering okay?"

"Yeah. Doc says she's doing great. And for the record, your daughter is pretty stubborn. It's an uphill battle to get her to take it easy."

"Kate does have a mind of her own." Candy smiled down at the sleeping baby. "It's good she's resting. I won't stay long."

"I'm sure she'll be awake soon and want to see you."

Candy glanced up, irony in her eyes. "I'm not so sure about that. Not that she'll be awake. The part where she's anxious to see me."

"You're her mother."

"Exactly. And I should have taken care of her."

Trying to translate that remark, Joe sat on the couch across from her. Did she think he was out of line? "I live close by and I'm here all the time to see J.T. She just needs a little help until she gets back on her feet."

"I don't mean now," Candy said. She glanced down at J.T. and brushed the hair off his sweaty forehead. "I meant when she was little. And even after that. Taking care of Kate should have been my job, but most of the time she acted like the grown-up and I behaved like the child every time I met a guy who promised me the moon."

"I'm sure she wants you to be happy." Man, he was way out of his league in this conversation.

"I kept trying. Wow, did I try. One of the men was abusive and Kate gave me an ultimatum—if I didn't get rid of him she was leaving."

Kate had never said anything about this. Had she gotten in the way, been hurt? "What happened?" he asked sharply.

"It shames me to say that I picked a man over my daughter. Especially when he walked out on me a month later. But the damage was done. Katie was on her own—not that she hadn't already *been* on her own."

It confirmed a lot of what Kate had told him, that she'd grown up too fast, without anyone to take care of her. But what Candy'd just admitted seriously ticked him off. How could you do that to your child? He understood a little better why Kate had thought long and hard before letting him know she was pregnant.

Still sleeping, J.T. moved his little mouth, as if he were

sucking, and tenderness welled up inside Joe along with grati-
tude for Kate's courage. She knew little about him except that
he was probably like all the guys she'd ever known who were
jerks. And if she hadn't written that letter, he would never have
known about his child or been able to be here to take care of him.

"Kids should come first," he said, hearing the edge to his voice.

Candy met his gaze, her own defensive. "No one is perfect."

"No one says you have to be."

"The words are politically correct, but you're judging me.
You try being a single mother. I had to do it alone after Katie's
father walked out on us. You're here now and I'm glad you're
taking responsibility for your son. I'm glad he's got a mom and
dad. I admit that I made mistakes that affected my daughter.
And you'll make mistakes that will affect your son."

She had no idea how hard he was trying not to hurt his son.
Considering what he'd done, even though it was during a time
of war, he was the last person on earth to judge anyone else.
But he couldn't stand the thought of Kate hurting, especially
as a child. This woman could have done better.

"All you had to do was put Kate's welfare above your
own," he said.

"So you think I'm a failure as a mother?" she asked, smiling
sadly at the little boy in her arms. She bent her head and gently
kissed his forehead.

"That's not what I said."

"I always thought loving my baby was the most important
thing. Maybe it was just a rationalization because I was a single
mom and couldn't be there all the time." She stared at Joe.
"You've been a father for what? Thirty seconds? Obviously I
was wrong about all of it."

She stood and walked around the coffee table to put his son
in his arms. Then she picked up her purse. "Obviously your

childhood was perfect and you've read the instruction book on fatherhood from cover to cover. But you need to know this, although you might not believe it." Her eyes grew intense. "I love my daughter more than anything in the world. I regret what she had to go through more than you'll ever know. I let every guy into my life hoping he was the one. Hoping for the best, but somehow I always got the worst. And my daughter watched me fall apart every time it didn't work out. It made her strong, but I'd give anything if I could undo the past, because being too strong isn't good for her. She doesn't let anyone in."

He'd told Kate more than once that she didn't have to be strong all the time. But if anyone knew how hard habits were to break, it was him.

He stood. "Look, Candy, I—"

"Obviously you don't think much of me, but I'd appreciate it if you'd tell Kate I stopped by," she said. She reached into her handbag and set a chocolate bar on the coffee table. "I'm glad she's feeling better."

She let herself out of the apartment and Joe thought about what she'd said. Everything he'd read on the subject confirmed that parenting was the most rewarding and toughest job you'd ever do. With J.T. he hadn't thought beyond the baby part. How would he hold up as a dad when his kid turned into a mouthy, rebellious teenager? Part of him wanted to deny that this sweet, innocent boy ever would, but he knew better. The kid had his DNA and as much as he hoped J.T. took after Kate, there was a fifty/fifty chance he'd challenge them both the way Joe had his folks.

And, just as Candy loved her daughter more than anything in this world, he knew he would love his son the same way. No matter what.

Which made him wonder. Had his father loved him like that? Maybe withholding praise had been his dad's way of motivating him to do better, to be the best he could be. God knows that's what Joe wanted for his son.

He wished he could talk to his father about his feelings now. Unfortunately he couldn't. What he did know was that fatherhood was forever, even though this interlude under Kate's roof was not.

She deserved a man without black marks on his soul. Black marks that were working their way out of his subconscious. The darkness of that nightmare had touched her after he'd touched her. And he was doing his damnedest not to do it again. If it happened again…

He ran his fingers through his hair. Like a good soldier, he'd hope for the best and plan for the worst. In the long run, spending this time with Kate and his son would cost him. When it was over he would always have a vision of what might have been.

If he was whole, he could promise Kate forever but he wasn't. And he would never pledge something unless he was certain he could deliver.

"I can't believe I slept so long. It's almost dinnertime." Yawning, Kate walked into the living room and plopped on the sofa, rubbing her eyes.

Joe was sitting in the glider chair, a brooding look on his face. "You must have needed the rest."

"Where's the baby?"

He finally looked at her. "Taking a nap."

She groaned. "That means he'll be up for the late-night talk shows."

As if he hadn't heard her he said, "Your mother stopped by."

She was running her fingers through her tousled hair and froze. "Mom was here? All the way from Pahrump?"

"Yeah. Said she was in the area. A doctor's appointment. Checkup. Nothing serious."

"Why didn't you wake me?"

"She said not to. Let you rest."

He linked his fingers over his flat abdomen. "She left something for you on the coffee table."

"A Heath Bar," she said without looking.

"Are you psychic?" His gaze narrowed. "How did you know that?"

She reached for the chocolate. "It's my favorite sweet thing in the whole world. Besides J.T.," she added, "I like them plain out of the wrapper, crushed up in vanilla ice cream or fat-free yogurt."

His mouth quirked up slightly. "Chocolate kind of cancels out the fat-free part, doesn't it?"

"In the best possible way," she agreed proudly.

"So how did you know that's what your mother left for you?"

"When I was a little girl, I was really sick. A cold or flu, I don't remember. But I was close to being admitted to the hospital. The doctor said I needed to eat and to push fluids. Mom tempted me with everything she could think of and brought me a Heath Bar. I loved it."

"Obviously you got better."

"Yeah. Without a hospital stay."

"Who knew chocolate-covered toffee had healing properties?"

"It's miraculous." She shrugged. "But ever since, if I wasn't feeling well, she brought me one."

"Every time?"

She nodded. "I didn't always tell her because she worried and there wasn't much money. But if she knew I was under the weather, I could count on her for candy to make me feel better. She always remembers."

Oddly enough, his frown deepened. "That's funny. From what she said, I got the impression she feels like she did everything wrong."

Kate started to feel bad. "What did she say?"

"That she had to believe loving you more than anything was enough because she couldn't be there all the time."

The words made Kate feel as if she'd been hit in the chest. "Are you sure it was *my* mom who said that?"

For a split second humor lit his eyes. "The woman looked a lot like you. A strong family resemblance."

"That's what everyone says."

"So you're telling me there were times she stepped up and was there for you?" He stared at her.

"Of course. Why?"

"Because the way you both talk, she's not a candidate for mother of the year."

"Doesn't every kid want their parent to be Ward or June Cleaver?"

"Mine weren't."

"Nobody's are," she said. "That's my point. And even if they were, kids would find something to complain about."

"Well, she got me thinking about things with my own father." Brooding Joe was back.

"I'll skip the part where I'm shocked that my mom could make you do that. But what are you thinking?"

He met her gaze. "About how I never felt I measured up in my dad's eyes. About how he probably loved me anyway but had a funny way of showing it. That's a different perspective for me because I never figured he cared at all."

"What did my mom say?"

"That she failed you. That you gave her an ultimatum and she picked a guy who walked out on her. She's ashamed about that, by the way."

Kate knew that, but a part of her still resented that time. "I can't believe she told you all that."

"It's because she wanted me to know how you got to be so strong. And why you're not good at letting people in when you need help."

If only chocolate and toffee could fix that problem, she would link arms and sing *Kumbaya* with the whole world. As it was, she'd learned to expect the worst of everyone she met and protect herself accordingly.

She wrapped her arms around a sofa throw pillow covered in brown and beige—warm earth tones that didn't make her feel warm at all. Darn it, she had good reasons for not wanting to let Joe Morgan in again. *Again* being the operative word.

"My issues are not breaking news," she said.

"No." He folded his arms over his chest. "But she had a point—we both love J.T. and want the best for him. In spite of that we're going to make mistakes just like our parents did. It made me think about how much I don't want to screw up our son."

"This may come as a surprise to you," she said, "but I don't wake up every morning and think about how I'm going to mess up J.T.'s life that day."

"That's not what I meant."

When he looked at her she saw the hungry, haunted expression he often wore, mostly when he thought she wasn't looking. Every time she felt as if he was trying to memorize a moment, a look on her face or the baby's, a laugh, a feeling, as if he was trying desperately to hang on to what he had. As if it would be ripped away.

She knew how it felt to lose someone she cared deeply for, and Joe Morgan was the man who'd taught her. It didn't matter any more that he'd had profoundly personal and painful reasons for what he'd done. She had to focus on not letting him do it to her again.

Every day, sometimes from minute to minute or second to

second, she fought to keep him out of her heart. After making love with him, it was like trying to counter a nuclear blast with a table fan. When she wasn't prepared, she'd glance at him and a yearning to kiss him, hold him, have him, would knot in her belly until it became a physical ache worse than anything she'd suffered post-surgery.

"I know you meant that you want the best for J.T.," she said. "My comment was a pathetic attempt at humor to make you feel better. There's a certain amount of truth to what my mom said. God knows I'm a product of my environment and so are you."

"Way to cheer me up. My father was a totalitarian dictator."

She shrugged. "As I see it, our obligation is to love our son, keep him safe, teach him the difference between right and wrong…we can only do our best."

"And buy out the parenting procedure manuals in every bookstore in Vegas." The brooding look disappeared when a slow smile curved his lips. "My pathetic attempt at humor to make you feel better."

That grin warmed her more than all the earth tones on earth. She was much safer when he brooded, although the bad boy look had something going for it, too. Damn him. He'd destroyed her once, taken all the color out of her world until she wondered if she'd ever see life in anything but shades of gray. It was not okay for him to make her hope for something that wasn't going to happen.

Now who was brooding?

A loud wail from the other room shattered the silence.

Without a word, Joe instantly stood up. It wasn't until she was staring at his broad back disappearing that Kate realized she hadn't moved. She hadn't immediately leapt into action for her child because instinctively she'd known he would.

She'd gone from letting him in under threat of legal action, to letting her guard down and counting on him. Somehow she had to get her game back on before it was too late. Put her defenses back in place. The only thing keeping her from making a fool of herself was that he'd shown no hint that he wanted her.

If he did, if he touched her in that way, looked at her as if he could devour her whole, no way would she be strong enough to resist letting him into her heart.

Chapter Twelve

Joe parked the SUV in front of Southwestern Helicopter Service and looked at Kate in the passenger seat beside him. The last time she'd come here with him, the visit had set in motion a chain reaction of events resulting in him talking about stuff he didn't even want to think about. That was before she'd scared the crap out of him with her appendicitis. Before he'd met her mother who'd made him face the fact that he was winging this parenthood thing just as his own father had.

He also remembered that the last time they were here Kate had told him in no uncertain terms that his son would always know he was loved because Joe would express his pride in J.T.'s accomplishments. For a guy who had wanted to hear such pride from his own dad, the advice was incredibly profound and deceptively easy.

"Okay, Slim," he said to her. "Let's get this over with."

"Aye, aye, sir," she said, saluting.

"Smart aleck."

They exited the SUV and Joe extracted their son from the rear seat. With J.T.'s car seat handle in one hand, Joe opened the office door with the other and let Kate go in ahead of him. When she stopped and bent over, putting a hand to her side, he felt that clutch of concern in his gut. He set the sleeping baby down by the metal desk nearest the door and turned to check her out.

"Are you okay?"

"Fine," she whispered.

"Maybe I should take you home," he said. "I knew this was a bad idea."

She straightened and flashed a wicked grin. "Gotcha."

He waited a moment for his adrenaline levels to return to normal, then said, "Has anyone ever mentioned that you've got a real mean streak?"

"Not mean. It's just too easy. And that was payback. It practically took an act of Congress to get permission to take a ride with you today. Just to check your work mail."

That was his own fault for letting it slip that paperwork was piling up and he was going to the office to triage the stack. She had pestered, persevered and pouted, but it hadn't been quite two weeks since her surgery. Then she'd taken her flair for drama out for a spin and come up with some song and dance about the walls closing in on her. Finally, he'd agreed to bring her along, although he wasn't happy. A good day for him was her safe at home where he could protect her. He never wanted to feel as helpless as he had when she'd been doubled over in pain.

So on the drive over here he'd fretted over every bump in the road. Each time he'd braked, he'd wondered if it was done smoothly enough, if he'd jarred her, hurt her.

"So sue me for being cautious," he said, glaring at her.

"Sue me for wanting some fresh air," she countered. "It

feels really good to breathe helicopter exhaust fumes and dust and see four different walls."

"Are you sure you're all right?" he asked.

She rolled her eyes. "If I had a quarter for every time you asked me that, I could retire a wealthy woman."

"Okay," he said, holding up his hands in surrender. "You've made your point. I'll back off."

But he wouldn't stop watching her. Partly because she was the best view in Vegas. Mostly because he couldn't help worrying about her, even though he'd given up the right.

Laura walked in from the back office and smiled. "Kate. How are you?"

She looked up and wrinkled her nose at him. "I got permission from the warden for a field trip."

"Sass," Laura said. "I like it. That means you must be feeling better."

"I'm not letting her stay out too long," Joe warned. "Just came by to check the mail and my messages."

"Good timing. I just put a stack of stuff on your desk."

"Okay." He started to lift the sleeping baby.

"I'll keep an eye on him," Laura said. "If I can handle you, this little guy is a piece of cake."

"Thanks." Then her words sank in. "I think."

He walked into his office with Kate following.

"I wanted to see the inner sanctum," she said. "Last time I didn't get a chance."

"It's no big deal. Basic. Utilitarian. If I didn't have a window that looked out on the airfield, the paperwork would drive me nuts."

"Because you'd rather be flying?" she asked.

"Yeah." He looked into her eyes, trying to decide if they looked more brown or hazel today.

Her eyes were a hot zone for him. He could get lost there, lose sight of the horizon and spin out of control. But a good pilot knew how to fly on instruments and evade trouble.

He turned his back. "I'm going to look through this stack. There's a chair by the desk. Use it."

"Yes, sir."

Without looking, he knew she'd saluted and couldn't help smiling. Laura was right. Sass meant she was fine. He was really good with fine.

He picked up the pile of envelopes and looked through them. His brother the bastard handled the legal part of the business and contracting with clients. Joe dealt with scheduling personnel, supplies and servicing their customers. Most of this mail was junk—soliciting for credit cards, magazines, ads for local sales.

With the scent of Kate's skin distracting him, he almost missed it. An envelope with the official Marine Corps logo.

He set the rest of the stuff down and ripped it open. Skimming the message, key words caught his eye—commendation, ceremony, request the honor of your presence. As if he needed this reminder of failure to kick up his guilt. It was always there, like an improvised explosive device that could go off at any time.

He tossed the paper on his desk beside the untouched mail and said, "Let's go."

When he turned around, Kate was not using the chair. On top of that she was staring at him. "What?" he asked.

"You didn't look at all of it," she pointed out.

"I need to get you home."

She shook her head. "Oh, please. Don't make this about me when you look like you just saw the ghost of Christmas past."

He wasn't sure what that would feel like, but it couldn't be as bad as what he was feeling right now. "I'm not the one who was in the hospital. Field trip is over."

"You're not finished."

"No, but I'm good." Big fat lie. "Looked at everything I need to. I think you've been out long enough for the first time."

He brushed past her and stopped in the doorway when he sensed she wasn't following. A paper rustling behind him put a knot in his gut and made him grit his teeth. When he turned back, he saw her resting a hip against his metal desk while reading the letter.

"Joe," she said, something close to reverence in her voice. "They're giving you a medal."

"Yeah."

"There's a ceremony," she said, pointing to the piece of paper. "This is a big deal."

"No, it's not."

She scanned it again. "They want you to be there."

"I'm not going."

"Why not?"

"No time. I've got a business to run. J.T. to take care of. Not to mention you."

"What about me?"

"Someone needs to save you from yourself—"

She pointed a finger at him. "Stop hiding behind me."

"If I needed cover, it would be someone bigger than you."

Why was it that every time she was here with him the past seemed to catch up and bite him in the ass?

"You're not going to distract me. What is this all about?"

"You really want to know?" he asked, glaring at her. "I don't want a damn medal."

"But you deserve it," she protested. "You're a hero—"

"Don't call me that."

"You served your country with distinction. I'm just stating a fact."

"The fact is I wasn't thinking about my country when that rocket-propelled grenade brought my chopper down. Or when they tied my hands behind my back and put a hood over my head."

Her face paled when she said, "Tell me what you *were* thinking about."

"Coming home. Not just the U.S.A. *Home.*"

It was more than that. It was about the son he'd never seen and how much he wanted to. He'd been remembering Kate and how damn much it had hurt to see the desolation in her eyes when he'd walked away from her because he hadn't known what else to do. He'd been thinking how badly he wanted to make it home and make it up to her.

"And you did come back," she reminded him. "But this letter says you could have saved yourself from the enemy. Instead you stayed with an injured comrade. You distinguished yourself and should be recognized for it."

He shook his head. "I survived. That's it. And my friend—"

"What about him?" She moved then, close enough to put her hand on his arm. "Tell me what happened?"

Not this time. He saw his own darkness reflected in her eyes—eyes that had lost any hint of green and had turned brown. At any cost he had to keep the past away from her. No way would he tell her what he'd had to do to survive and, even worse, that he was responsible for a soldier's death.

"No."

She flinched and her eyes widened. "No?"

"I don't want to talk about it."

She stared at him for a long time, then finally nodded. "Okay. Let's go home."

Shadows filled her eyes, clear evidence that she was troubled by his refusal to confide in her. He hated that he'd taken all the sass out of her. It hurt as bad as the day he'd told her they were over. But he had no choice now any more than he'd had then. Not if he was going to protect her. She'd told him doing the best you could was always right. Without a doubt he knew protecting her was the best thing he could do.

"So, I'm cleared by the doctor to go back to work." In the passenger seat of Joe's SUV, Kate glanced at him as they pulled out of the medical building's lot on Horizon Ridge Parkway. "It's official. You have no good reason to be a helicopter guy."

When he looked at her, she knew that behind his sexy aviator sunglasses there would be an expression in his eyes that said she needed a different doctor—the kind who could decide whether or not she was crazy.

"I *am* a helicopter guy," he pointed out far too rationally.

"Haven't you ever heard the term *helicopter mom?* It refers to mothers who hover around their kids all the time."

"No."

"Well, you've been hovering since my surgery and now it's officially time to give it a rest. You no longer have any reason to ask if I'm okay or how I feel."

"Understood."

She kept stealing sideways looks at him, feeling the urge to memorize the strength in his jaw, the hollow in his cheek, the laugh lines around his eyes. She needed to hang on to the small things and hold them close. Since that day in his office everything felt fragile and finite.

"That's it?" she asked. "Understood?"

When there was an opening in traffic, he turned right and stopped at the light. He glanced over. "It means I get what you're saying."

During her medical crisis he hadn't been so taciturn. Was

he feeling it, too? That everything was about to change? Now that she was cleared to resume normal life, Joe could do the same. He'd move back to his place and she'd stay put. Alone.

The problem was she'd gotten used to having him around and kind of liked that he was a helicopter guy. In her whole life she'd never had anyone hover. She just wished he would let her return the favor. In the last ten days she'd given him openings to talk about what had happened to him overseas. He was as good at evading conversation as he was at hovering.

"Would you mind if we stop at the store before we pick up J.T. at Marilyn's? I just need a couple of things and it will be faster." They'd decided the doctor's appointment would go more smoothly if the baby wasn't with them.

"No problem. I called to check on him while you were in the exam room and he'd just gone down for his afternoon nap."

"Okay. Good."

He turned left on Eastern Avenue, then made a quick right into the supermarket lot. He grabbed a basket when they went inside, then pushed it while Kate threw in disposable diapers, moist wipes, baby food, milk, bread, coffee and laundry soap. It felt incredibly ordinary and terribly domestic. And profoundly sad because they weren't a couple. Just a man and woman co-parenting.

"That's all I can think of," she said.

"Roger that."

Why did the military jargon turn her on so much? She stole another glance at him. In his snug T-shirt and worn jeans, he was hotter than the Vegas Valley on the Fourth of July. They scanned everything at self-checkout and she was surprised the heat she was generating didn't short it out. When there was a total, Joe reached for his wallet.

"I'll get it," she said.

"Negative." He looked down. "Trust me on this. It's a guy thing."

"Translation, arm-wrestling for purchasing rights is out of the question?"

He just grinned and put his card in the slot.

When they got back to the apartment complex, Joe still wouldn't let her carry anything heavier than a loaf of bread. But that wasn't about hovering. He'd always been a gentleman. It was one of the things that had attracted her from the beginning.

She stood in the doorway to the kitchen and leaned a shoulder against the wall, watching him put away the groceries. Emotions swirled through her and a deep sadness took hold. "Joe?"

"Hmm?"

Why did he look so darn sexy, so incredibly handsome with his sunglasses hanging from the neck of his T-shirt and dark hair mussed in that trendy, masculine way? What was it about this man that grabbed hold of her and wouldn't let go?

"I just wanted to thank you for everything."

He straightened slowly and frowned. "What are you talking about?"

"What part of *thank you* isn't clear?" She lifted one shoulder in a shrug. "I appreciate that you picked up the slack while I was recuperating. You were here for me and I'm very grateful."

"Are you trying to get rid of me?"

"No!" She shook her head. "God, no. I don't know what I'd have done if you hadn't been here. It's just—"

"What?"

"I don't— We've been—" She wanted to ask where they went from here. There was a part of him he refused to share and she couldn't make him. Just as troubling was the fact that he hadn't touched her or even hinted that he'd wanted her, not since the night he'd made love to her just a few feet from where they stood now. "You haven't—"

"I haven't what?"

She didn't know how to say this and was sorry she'd brought it up. Her body might be ready to resume normal activity, but clearly her brain needed more time.

"Never mind," she said.

He moved closer and his eyes narrowed. "No. You don't get to do that."

"What? Not talk?"

"Yeah."

"So it's okay for you to shut down, but I have to spill my guts?"

"You don't get to start a sentence that way and not tell me what I haven't done."

She searched his gaze and all the need that had built up inside her pushed against her heart. "You've been here for weeks, but you haven't touched me since the night we went to dinner."

"Kate—" Her name came out in a tormented groan.

"I'm sorry. I didn't mean to put you on the spot. It's okay. I appreciate that you've been here—"

"I've been here all right," he said, his voice harsh. "I've been here every damn night fighting like hell to keep my hands off you."

She blinked. "You have?"

"The only reason I haven't kissed the living daylights out of you is because you were recovering from surgery."

"Really?" Joy as bright as the lights on the Las Vegas Strip poured through her.

He reached for her and dragged her against him, folding her into his arms. "Really—"

His gaze skipped over her face for a long moment before he shook his head in self-disgust, as if he'd lost some kind of battle. Then he touched his mouth to hers, tasting, teasing, testing. Heat balled inside her and set her nerve endings on fire. It burned even after he tore his lips from hers and buried his face in her hair.

"I'm the one who should be thanking you," he said, his breathing fast and uneven when he met her gaze. "Being here— With you— It's like a safe haven."

"From what?" she asked, searching his face, seeing the shadows in his eyes.

"The darkness. The demons." He pulled her close and his breath stirred her hair.

"Joe—" She slid her arms around his waist and held on as tightly as she could. "I want to be there for you the way you've been here for me. Let me—"

"You have been. You don't get it, do you?" He rubbed his chin over the top of her head. "With you—here… This is the only place I go where I can keep them from following."

"Talk to me—"

He laughed harshly. "That's the last thing I want."

"Then tell me what you want."

"You." He took her face gently in his palms and stared into her eyes. "I've been trying not to. Trying to be noble. But I want you so much it's ripping me up inside. I'm going to a deeper level of hell, but I'll shake hands with the devil himself if I can have you just one more time."

She didn't smile on the outside, but inside there was a huge grin. "That's all I needed to know."

Kate stood on tiptoe and touched her mouth to his. For a second, he froze, then a moan tore up from his chest as his arms came around her and locked her to him. She'd started this, but Joe took command like the warrior he was. And for this oasis in time, she let herself need all of his safe male strength.

He angled her body against his and kissed her hard, almost

desperately. He took her lips until they softened, parted, invited. A man of action, he didn't hesitate to slip his tongue inside to duel with hers, an erotic dance designed to seduce. The maneuver worked with pathetic ease and was deliciously successful.

Just like that she couldn't seem to draw enough air into her lungs. Her chest rose and fell as if she'd run up and down the stairs a dozen times. And her heart... Pressed to him, she could feel Joe's heart beating, too, pounding against hers.

After plundering her mouth, he turned his amazing powers of concentration to her nose, eyes, cheeks, jaw and neck. He sucked gently on an exquisitely sensitive spot just beneath her ear. When an involuntary moan of sheer pleasure escaped, he smiled and blew softly on the dampness, sending shivers of sensation shimmering down her spine.

At the same time his hands were sliding and skimming over her back as he turned her in a circle. Her mind was muzzy from his assault on her senses and it didn't register at first that he'd waltzed her into her bedroom.

She slid her hands across his broad shoulders. "You're good, Joe."

"What?" he asked, all phony innocence.

"That was a sneak attack."

His grin was sinfully seductive and extraordinarily sexy. "I haven't done anything yet."

"That's where you're wrong. You've lit my fire," she said, sliding her tongue over her lips.

His grin disappeared, replaced by an intensity that took her breath away. The next thing she knew they were beside the bed. She was frantically tugging his T-shirt from the waistband of his jeans. He whipped it off and tossed it aside. With a growl of frustration, he abandoned the tiny buttons on her blouse, grabbed the hem and pulled it over her head. Shorts, panties, bra quickly followed and he took his sweet time looking. His eyes, his smile, the expression on his face were pure and simple male appreciation.

He traced a gentle finger over the swell of one breast, then the other. "Beautiful."

Straightforward sincerity and the highest praise she could ever want melted her heart and sent liquid heat coursing through her.

She rested her palms on his chest. "You, too."

The dusting of hair tickled her hands and she dragged them across the contour of muscle, down his abdomen. When she stopped just above the jeans slung low on his hips, he sucked in a breath, then mimicked her actions. He traced her stomach and a muscle jumped as she drew in air.

Need stabbed through her, insistent—demanding. She yanked the comforter down, then crawled onto the sheets, savoring the coolness on her heated skin.

Stretched out on her side, raised up on an elbow, she sent him a look. "You're overdressed."

He set his expression on sizzle then slowly unbuckled his belt, slid down jeans and boxers and let his erection spring free. Like a predator, he loomed over her then eased her onto her back and kissed her deeply, seductively. Sliding down, he turned his attention to her breasts, first one then the other. Heat sparked inside her—growing, twisting, curling.

When she thought she couldn't possibly bear the pleasure any longer, he moved to her belly, stroking with his tongue, then breathing on the moisture. Her flesh tingled and she started to tremble in the best way. He drew a finger over the recently healed scar on her lower right side and his eyes went dark before he kissed it, fiercely tender.

She moaned and threaded her fingers in his hair. When he met her gaze, she took his face in her hands and brought his mouth to hers. All the feelings inside her that she couldn't put into words she put into that kiss. Tenderly, she touched her lips to the jagged scar on his chin that hadn't been there before he left her.

They both had scars.

And they both had now.

She looked into his eyes and knew that what was in hers matched the intensity she saw in his. The hardest words for her to say came with surprising ease.

"I need you, Joe."

Once a marine, always a marine—and prepared. He took care of protection, then settled himself between her legs and slowly slid inside her, hot and hard, the weight of him solid and strong. At first slow, his thrusts were deep and sensual. Her hips moved with him, finding the rhythm as it grew faster. The sounds of their labored breathing mingled and filled the room just as he filled her body. And her soul.

As the heat grew in her belly, she arched her back and drew him deep as a cry of pleasured release scraped its way from her throat. Shattering into a thousand points of light, she clung to him and heard his groan. He tensed and held her, burying his face in her hair as he found his own satisfaction.

Eyes closed and, too relaxed to open them, she felt the bed dip as Joe left her. She missed his weight and the feel of his bare skin against hers.

When he returned to bed, he gathered her to him, snuggling her to his side. "So, how do you feel?"

Kate heard the laughter in his question and knew he was re-membering that after leaving the doctor's office she'd warned him never to ask again. "I've never felt better in my life."

"Good."

"How do you feel?"

"Like I died and went to heaven."

Like the Joe he'd been before he left her, she thought. It had been pathetically easy for him to make her want what they'd had then. But sex had never been their problem. His walking away without an explanation was what she had a hard time forgiving. If he'd told her what had happened with his wife, she'd have understood. She wouldn't have been happy, but she'd have understood.

She was here now, content in his arms because she'd thrown caution to the wind and let him know what she wanted. She'd taken a risk. He wasn't a mind reader and neither was she. If he didn't talk to her about the demons he'd mentioned, they would follow him here and stand between them.

She didn't know what he'd gone through in Afghanistan, but whatever it was had torn him up and wouldn't let him heal.

"Joe?" She tilted her head back and looked at him.

He dropped a quick kiss on her mouth. "Hmm?"

"Tell me about the darkness. The demons. What happened to you over there?"

His whole body went rigid. "It's in the past. Forget it. I have."

"That's not what you said before."

"I can't be responsible for what I say when you're in my arms. You mess with my mind and short circuit all the connections to my brain."

"I'd be flattered," she said, "if I didn't know that you're trying to distract me."

"Is it working?"

"No."

He slid her out of his arms, then rolled away. "I promised myself that the bad stuff would stay over there. Don't ask me to bring it here—to you, to our son—and taint what I have now."

When he put it like that, how could she push, even though the need to help him was an ache deep inside? She knew that as surely as she knew the sun just setting would rise again tomorrow. Whatever darkness he kept inside had to come out because it was in his subconscious, clawing and scraping its way to the light. But he'd shut her down, closed her out, even more than he had when he'd walked away without telling her why.

He'd just given her his body and the greatest pleasure she'd ever known, but he wouldn't trust her with his soul and that hurt more than anything. If only she could close off her own escalating feelings as easily as he could, because she could never completely shut him out of her life.

They shared a son and Joe was dedicated to being the best father he could be. It would involve talking, listening, sharing. It meant seeing him and knowing she could never have what she truly wanted.

That was a level of pain she wasn't sure it was possible to manage.

Chapter Thirteen

Kate walked down the now-familiar hall in the office building on the corner of Eastern Avenue and Mercy Medical Center Parkway. Her sandals made no sound on the gray carpet before she stopped at the impressive double doors bearing the name-plate Preston Morgan, Attorney-at-Law. She shifted the car seat from one hand to the other, remembering vividly the day she'd come here six months pregnant, still heartbroken, and not entirely convinced she was doing the right thing.

She looked at her son and realized the only difference was that she was carrying the baby in her hand instead of her belly.

"You're getting heavy, big guy. I think you should carry me."

His response was baby babble that normally made her smile, but not today. "We're going to see your Uncle Preston."

He stuck his brightly colored plastic keys in his mouth and stared up at her, blue eyes big and wide.

"I don't know what else to do. Daddy doesn't want to taint

what he already has, but he's doing that by not talking to Mommy about what's bothering him." He banged his toy on his belly then shook the keys and laughed. "Right. Let's go shake things up."

She opened the door to the plush waiting room. Textured green paper covered the walls and complemented the mahogany tables. Several leather chairs were arranged in a semicircle across from a seafoam-green sofa, making a pleasant conversation area. That was a good start. Conversation was her ultimate goal.

She walked over to the information desk. "I'd like to see Preston—Mr. Morgan," Kate amended.

The young woman glanced up, showing big, gorgeous, intelligent gray eyes. Somewhere in her late twenties, she was incredibly attractive with long, thick, shiny brown hair. Her curves were in all the right places, although some would call her plump. The nameplate in front of her read Jordan Foster.

"Do you have an appointment?" she asked.

"No." Kate set the car seat on the luxurious hunter-green carpet. "If he's busy, I can wait."

"Your name, please?"

"Kate Carpenter." She looked down at the baby. "And J. T. Morgan, Preston's nephew."

Jordan Foster's eyes widened slightly, but that was the only hint that she was the least bit surprised. "Have a seat. I'll see if he's available."

Kate was too jittery to sit and paced the room, glancing at seascapes on the walls. J.T. looked around curiously, then arched his back and pushed against the restraining chest and lap straps, a big clue that the window of happy time in the car seat was just about to slam shut. When he started grunting and his face turned red, there was no doubt what he was doing.

"Oh, buddy," she groaned. "You so need to work on your timing."

He just grinned, showing off four teeth—two on the top, two on the bottom. She needed to change him, but decided to wait until the receptionist came back and told her to go away and come back when she had an appointment.

Just then the door to the back office opened and Preston was there, looking very lawyerly and handsome in his navy pin-striped slacks, white dress shirt and red tie. Joe's ex-wife might have been after money, but her taste in men was impeccable. The Morgans were heartbreaker material. Her son not so much just yet, she thought when she caught a whiff of the present he'd made, and wrinkled her nose.

"Kate," Preston said, smiling. "This is a pleasant surprise."

She studied the expression on his handsome face and decided if he was lying about being pleased it was a darn fine act. "I apologize for disturbing you in the middle of your work day."

"Practicing law isn't quite as exciting as TV and the movies would like you to think. I'm grateful for the break." He looked down when J.T. let out a whimper, then squatted down in front of him. "And grateful to see this little guy."

"You won't say that if the wind changes."

He looked up. "Excuse me?"

"He needs to be changed."

"Come into my office," he offered.

"Not a good idea. Trust me." She cocked her thumb over her shoulder toward the hall. "There was a ladies' room on the way in. We'll just go there and…"

"No way." He slid the diaper bag from her shoulder. "If you've got the supplies, I've got the space."

"And a heavy-duty ventilation system?" she asked.

"I'm tough." He grabbed the car seat and carried it down the hall to his office, leaving her no choice but to follow. After walking in, he set the baby down. "He's heavy."

"I was just telling him the same thing." She looked around at the exquisite collection of orange, cobalt-blue and green glassware, feeling very awkward and out of her element. "Look, Preston, it's very nice of you to let me change him in here, but it just feels wrong."

"He's my nephew, Kate. A Morgan. A manly man. What feels wrong is to take him to the ladies' room." He smiled wryly. "I can't be responsible for giving him issues."

She laughed. "You're sure?"

"Very."

"Remember, this was your idea," she said, releasing the straps on the squirming baby.

After arranging the pad to set him on, wipes and a fresh diaper, she went to work. Preston waited a discreet distance away, leaning back against one of the chairs in front of his desk.

"How've you been, Kate?"

"Fine—other than a recent appendectomy," she said, glancing up.

He frowned. "Are you okay?"

She smiled, remembering Joe constantly bugging her about that very thing. The last time was after he'd loved the living daylights out of her. She'd felt pretty darn fine until he'd shut down communications.

"I'm great. Back to work. I'm off today," she explained.

"I guess everything worked out while you were under the weather?" He folded his arms over his chest.

"Yeah. Joe took care of everything."

"Good." He looked down for a moment. "You know I'm here if you need anything."

"Thanks. And it has to be said—funny you should mention that."

"Oh?" One dark eyebrow arched.

"I thought it was about time you had a visit with your nephew." She undid the diaper fasteners and lifted J.T.'s legs then cleaned him off. When the dirty diaper was neatly folded, bagged and stashed for disposal in the ladies' room, she set his bottom on the clean diaper and secured it.

"I'm glad you did." He paused, then said, "Don't take this wrong, but it's so sudden."

She glanced up from refastening J.T.'s shorts. She knew now the details behind Joe's beef with his brother, but she wasn't getting a vibe that Preston was hitting on her. Just the opposite. How many guys would be okay with dirty diaper-changing in their work space?

"You're right." She stood the baby up on his sturdy legs and held his chubby hands. "It's about Joe. He finally told me what happened between you."

"I see." Preston didn't look happy.

The baby sat down then crawled away and Kate leaned back on her heels, staring up at his uncle. "Is that all you have to say?"

"He told you I slept with his wife. What else is there to say?"

"I'm not sure. Except I can't shake the feeling that there's more to it."

"For every cause of action there's a point of view," he said.

She waited but he didn't say more. "What does that mean?" she finally asked.

"There are two sides to the story, but my brother only listened to one."

When the baby grabbed his slacks and stood, Preston bent to pick him up. He smiled when J.T. poked a chubby finger at the knot of his tie, probably the first neckwear he'd ever seen, since Joe rarely put one on.

"What's your side of the story?" she asked.

"No offense, Kate, but that's between me and my brother." He looked at the baby, a sad wistful expression on his face. "He refuses to listen and has made it clear there won't be a relationship between us."

Every instinct she had told her that this problem with Preston was the key to opening Joe up. "And you're okay with that? Don't you want to work this out?"

"It doesn't seem to matter to him what I want." He set the boy down when he started to squirm, but J.T. held onto his leg and Preston reached down a hand to steady him.

"That's not an answer, you know."

He shrugged. "I'm a lawyer. We don't give straight answers."

She studied him: the handsome face, the shadows in his blue eyes. What was it about the Morgan men and their tendency to go to the dark side? Darn it, she didn't want that for J.T. and they were going there if something didn't change with Joe.

"Okay. I'll stop asking questions if you'll do me a favor."

"Like I said before, if you ever need anything—"

"Talk to Joe."

"Anything but that," he said.

"You haven't heard what it's about yet."

"Doesn't matter. He won't talk to me."

"He needs to open up to someone." When the baby crawled toward the armoire with its brightly colored glass, she stood up and moved closer—to grab him if necessary. "I think he went through a lot of trauma while he was overseas. He pretends he's fine, but he had a nightmare when we—" Were sleeping together? Not going there. "Something's troubling him. And he hinted at things then shut down when I asked him about it."

"What makes you think he'll open up to me?"

"You're a guy. More important, you're his brother."

"Like I said, he doesn't see it that way any more."

When J.T. reached and missed a crystal bud vase on the bottom shelf, she swooped him into her arms. "There was a bond once. That must count for something."

"In his mind it's broken."

"And in yours?"

He frowned. "I thought you were going to stop asking questions."

"You haven't agreed to talk to Joe."

One corner of his mouth quirked up. "When you went into nursing, it was a tragic loss for the legal community."

That was another thing he and Joe both did well—distracting with humor. Whether these two stubborn men wanted to admit it or not, they had a lot in common. If she was as adept as Preston implied, she could get him to take what was left of their brotherly bond out for one last spin.

"Your father was responsible for steering Joe toward the military. And he distinguished himself in the service of his country."

"You'll get no argument from me."

"But why should that service cost him a chance at a fulfilling life?"

"Aren't you being overly dramatic?"

"No." She set the baby back in his car seat and hooked him in before he could wiggle free. When he let out a squeal, she handed him his keys and he put them in his mouth. She stood and met Preston's gaze. "If someone doesn't get through to Joe and convince him to talk about what happened to him, I think the blackness will suck him in."

He nodded, but it was the kind of nod that meant he heard, but didn't plan to argue further. "I'll think about what you said."

She was sure that wasn't a lie. There was no doubt in her mind that he'd remember this conversation, but she hadn't gotten the promise she was after—a commitment to an emotional intervention from the only family member who could help. Defeat was a bitter, frustrating, painful thing.

"Thanks for listening, Preston." She met his gaze. "I just can't help feeling that you're his last hope."

"He's got you. That makes him one of the lucky ones."

Did Joe really have her? Had she given her heart back to the man who'd already walked away once and returned to shut her out?

"Good-bye." She picked up the car seat.

He moved forward. "Let me carry him out for you."

"No thanks. I can do it by myself."

Just as she always did. She'd broken her own rule and reached out for help. A turn-down shouldn't really surprise her. If there was any silver lining to the baggage of her past, it was determination. She would find a way to help Joe because she couldn't find a way to stop caring about him.

Joe was tired to the bone. The couch in Kate's living room didn't lend itself to a good night's sleep, but that was probably just as well. Dozing helped him control the nightmares.

He stood by the apartment complex community barbecue and flipped the burgers. After wrapping his fingers around his longneck, he tipped the bottle to his mouth and took a long swallow. It was still hot in August, but there was hope for a cool-off soon.

He meant the weather, because Kate had already cooled off. Since that afternoon a week ago when she'd put his temptation to the test and he'd failed, she'd been withdrawn. To be fair, it was about his refusal to discuss the past, but today he'd noticed the change even more. Ever since she'd got home late that afternoon from wherever she'd gone, she'd been quiet. Distracted. Preoccupied.

Distant.

He was no Dr. Phil, but he wasn't an idiot. This was about what he'd let slip before making love to her. Later, when his brain rebooted and his cylinders weren't firing on pure testosterone, he'd kicked himself for what he'd said. Even more, he kicked himself for shutting her down. He knew she needed the emotional connection. But she wanted it with the man she remembered and he wasn't that man.

War had changed him.

What he'd seen and done made him different and he couldn't really fit in with normal people. He flipped the burgers again and pressed them with the long-handled spatula. Everyday things like barbecuing burgers didn't make him a normal guy.

He was here because of Kate's medical emergency, and he'd already stayed too long. But every time he tried to make himself go, he was afraid that he'd lose the little bit of normal still left inside him.

After sliding the burgers onto a plate, he walked through the complex and back upstairs, letting himself into the apartment.

"Dinner is served," he said, putting the food on the table in the dining room. In the high chair, J.T. squealed at the sight of him and he dropped a kiss on the boy's head.

Kate looked up from slicing a tomato. "Okay. Everything's ready."

No squeal of delight from her.

She brought the relish plate over and set it down before

giving the baby a couple of pieces of banana to keep him busy while they ate. Without another word, she sat and started to assemble her hamburger.

He took the seat to her right, on the other side of the baby. "How was your day?"

"Fine. Yours?"

"Busy. I flew a patient in from Pahrump. A woman went into labor early. High-risk pregnancy."

"Oh?"

He nodded. "There was an accident on Blue Diamond Road that closed it to through traffic. There's another route to the hospital but it adds forty-five minutes to the trip. They called Southwestern Helicopter for transport."

"Good."

He waited several moments, waiting for questions. Were the mother and baby okay? Boy or girl? The usual things she would ask. But she didn't say a word while she pulled her hamburger bun apart. The hairs on the back of his neck stood up, some warning system left over from the hot zone, and he couldn't shake the feeling that something bad was about to happen. This would be a good time for Kate to turn on the sunshine.

"What did you do today?" he asked.

She met his gaze. "I don't think you really want to know."

"I wouldn't have asked if I didn't," he answered, even as warning signals screamed in his head.

"I went to see your brother."

Shoots and scores, he thought, his gut knotting with anger. He'd made his feelings about that pretty clear. So what was going on? "Was there a particular reason for your visit?"

"Yes." She looked at him, her expression challenging.

"Are you going to tell me what it was?"

"I have nothing to hide."

That was no information at all. "It never occurred to me you did."

"Oh, please, Joe. The look on your face tells me exactly what you thought."

He'd have to work on that, but figured it was a losing battle where Kate was concerned. He cared. Damn it. Somehow the feelings ambushed him and as hard as he tried to push them back, he couldn't gain any ground. He cared about her and didn't want her with his brother.

"Tell me I'm wrong."

She rolled her eyes. "I took J.T. to see his uncle. And before you say anything, hear me out. Preston is your brother and it's my opinion that he has the right to see his nephew. They're family."

"In spite of what he did to me?"

"Stop being so stubborn and listen to his side of the story. You told him off and he should be able to defend himself. That's how communication works. Listening and talking."

He was sorry he'd opened his mouth and asked about her day. The anger churning in his gut told him it was time to shut down this conversation. "Understood."

"That wasn't the only reason I went to see him," she said, clearly not ready to cease and desist. "I asked him to talk to you."

"We have nothing to say."

"It's obvious you have a lot to say, but not to me. I thought he could—" She ignored the smear of banana J.T. left on her forearm. "It seems to me you need to confide in someone. Another guy. Preston is family." She shrugged. "So I asked."

Joe hated that he was even the slightest bit curious about his brother's response but couldn't hold back the question. "What did he say?"

"That he was the last person you wanted to see. But he agreed to think about it."

Joe stood up. "I can't believe you did that after I told you what happened and *communicated* that I didn't want you anywhere near him."

Kate pushed her plate away. When the baby started to whimper, she removed the high-chair tray, undid the seat belt and lifted him out. Settling him on her hip, she kissed J.T., then looked at him. "I understand you want to protect me. And your son. But here's the thing, Joe. You don't get to tell me who I can and can't see. You can't butt into my life and tell me to stay out of yours. I might be a screwed-up mess who has trouble letting people in, but you do the same thing. In fact, you've turned it into an Olympic event and brought home the gold medal."

He ran his fingers through his hair. "Kate, I—"

"Forget it." She shifted the fussy baby to her other hip. "I'm going to give him a bath."

They stared at each other for several moments—a classic standoff. He'd brought something home all right, but it wasn't a medal. The bad stuff was infiltrating and soon it would blow up in his face, rip his fairy tale to shreds.

Kate looked at him with the same expression she'd worn the first night he walked back into her life. As though she expected him to run out on her. As though she didn't trust him. The fact that she was right to be wary didn't make him hate that look any less now than he had then.

Chapter Fourteen

Kate flipped her pillow over, then punched it.

She glanced at her digital clock and noted it was 2:10 a.m.—five minutes later than the last time she'd checked. She tossed and turned some more, wondering how she could feel so cold when it was still over ninety degrees outside. The answer was easy. The bed felt bigger, lonelier and colder without Joe. He had never shared it with her. At least not for sleeping. That was part of the problem, since the memories of making love wouldn't let her rest.

It was especially cold after their fight earlier. Maybe if he'd gone home after the doctor had pronounced her fit for duty the fight could have been avoided. But he hadn't left, and she couldn't bring herself to ask why. She should tell him to go, except after having him there, alone was a dark and lonely place she couldn't bear to live in. After the things they'd said to each other earlier, she'd expected him to be gone after J.T.'s bath. Wrong. He'd stuck around. He'd been brooding, but he wasn't gone.

She refused to be sorry that she'd seen his brother and hiding it was counterproductive to her goal. Communication was the cornerstone of a relationship. Secrets undermined that cornerstone. But two-way interaction—her talking and him answering—was pretty much necessary, which made what they had a non-relationship. Facing that made her cold deep down inside, in a place Joe had set on fire once, a corner of her soul she'd been so certain she'd sealed off. But the hurt that crept in with the cold was proof that she'd let him in again. It was only possible to hurt this much if…

There was a noise from the living room. Her door was ajar so she could hear J.T. during the night, but all was quiet from his room across the hall. The sounds weren't coming from there. It was Joe in the living room, mumbling and thrashing.

She threw back the sheet and swung her legs over the side of the bed. In tank top and a pair of sweat shorts, she went to the door and listened. The incoherent muttering grew louder and she was afraid he'd wake the baby.

In the living room, outside security lights from the apartment complex filtered through the blinds. She could clearly see Joe, his big body curved to fit the too-small couch. Clad only in boxers, he tossed and turned on the ill-fitting sheet covering the cushions. His pillow was on the floor. Biting her lip uncertainly, she wondered whether the restlessness would pass without intervention.

"No!" he cried out.

The outburst startled her and she jumped, heart hammering against the inside of her chest. Clearly she had to wake him before he woke J.T.

She moved beside him. "Joe?" she whispered.

He was breathing hard and sweat glistened on his skin, but he didn't respond.

"Wake up, Joe," she said, gently touching his shoulder.

It happened so fast she didn't have time to make a sound. One second she was bent over him, the next she was flat on her back. The forearm he pressed against her neck cut off her startled squeal along with oxygen. Before her vision grew fuzzy, she saw a Joe she'd never seen. She got a good look at the intensity of the warrior on the offensive before stars danced in front of her eyes.

"Joe," she managed to gasp. "It's me. Kate."

"Kate?"

A heartbeat later his arm moved, pressure eased, and she choked out a cough before dragging in air.

Joe grasped her shoulders and helped her to a sitting position. "Kate? What are you doing?"

"You were having a nightmare." She ran a shaky hand through her hair. "I didn't want you to wake the baby. I—I just touched you to—snap you out of it."

"Did I hurt you?" When she didn't answer right away, he said more sharply, "Are you okay?"

"I'm fine," she whispered. "No harm done."

He'd startled her. Threw her ass over teakettle onto her back and pinned her there, but she wasn't damaged. Physically.

"Oh, God— Kate—"

He sank down on the couch, careful not to let any part of him be in contact with her, shame mixing with horror in his eyes. Resting his elbows on his knees, he lowered his head and linked his fingers behind his neck.

She put her hand on his arm, feeling the warm, slick skin. "Joe, it's okay—"

"No." He flinched away from her touch and lifted his troubled gaze to hers. "It's not okay. It will never *be* okay."

"It was a bad dream. That's all."

"All?" he said derisively. "You should have stayed away. I could have hurt you."

"But you didn't. I want to help—"

"You can't help. Don't you get it? I'm not the guy you knew before. I'm never going to be that guy again."

She didn't understand, and his self-loathing ripped her apart. She could only think of one thing to say to make him stop, to make it better. "I love you."

He went completely still. "What?"

"I loved you the first time we were together. And this guy you are now? I love him, too."

"Hanging out with my brother is a funny way of showing it."

"He's not your enemy," she said.

He laughed but it was an ugly, hollow sound. "Let it go, Kate."

"I can't."

He shot her a glare, then shook his head. "Why can't you forget it?"

"Because you can't," she said gently. "I know you don't understand, but it's why I went to see your brother."

"In some wars it's not so easy to know who the enemy is." He stood and walked across the room, then turned back.

"There's no war in this room. Just you and me, and I'm on your side."

He whirled to face her. "It won't work. It won't help. There's nothing you can do—"

"I can't if you won't let me. Tell me what's wrong."

"What's wrong?" He blew out a long breath. "It would be easier to tell you what isn't wrong."

"Then tell me what happened," she begged.

Unconsciously he brushed his thumb over the scar on his chin. Finally he nodded. "I choppered into a hot zone to extract a Special Forces team doing recon in an isolated area of Afghanistan. Just after going airborne with everyone safe and sound, there was an explosion. We'd been hit by an RPG and the chopper started to buck and pitch. I couldn't control it. The best I could do was a real hard landing."

"Oh, Joe—"

"We were pinned down by enemy fire," he continued as if he hadn't heard her. His face took on a faraway expression and he wasn't with her any longer, but back there. In the desert. A war on the other side of the world. "I tried to radio for help, but the equipment was too badly damaged. We held on but the bastards could smell blood in the water and kept circling. More and more kept coming."

"What did you do?" she prompted when he hesitated.

"One of the men was injured and couldn't make a run for it. Our only hope was to hold them off while the others went for help. I stayed behind, waiting for the rescue team to get there. But we ran low on ammunition."

If a rescue team had arrived, he would have made it home a lot sooner. When he showed up on her doorstep out of the blue all he'd said was that his helicopter was shot down and the Taliban extended their hospitality for a while.

"You were captured." It wasn't a question.

His mouth thinned to a grim line. "Yeah."

"They didn't send help?"

"I'm sure a squad was dispatched, but we'd already been removed from that location. No doubt they searched, but it was like finding a needle in a haystack. Too much desert, too many mountains. Not enough intel."

"You're here. It seems like I heard that when captured your mission is to escape. Obviously you were successful."

"It wasn't worth the price."

The tortured look on his face made her sorry she'd asked, but she'd started this and it wasn't fair to stop now. "Joe?" When he shook his head, she asked, "What price?"

"Private first class Mark Robertson."

"The injured soldier?"

He nodded. "We'd been held prisoner a couple of days and I had a plan to get out. He insisted he was okay and could keep up. After bribing a guard to look the other way, we slipped out of the village, but the guard blew the whistle. They caught up with us. And—" He swallowed hard. "I told them it was all me. My idea. My responsibility. Take it out on me."

"What did they do to you?" She was afraid to hear, but more afraid he wouldn't tell her.

"Nothing."

"What?"

"They didn't do anything to me. Except force me to watch them put a bullet in Robbie's head."

"Oh, God—"

"The only reason they didn't kill me, too, is that I had value as a hostage. Possible ransom. Like the government would give them money to finance more terror." He was breathing hard and rage burned in his eyes. "But they say success is the best revenge. So I watched and waited."

"For what?"

"A chance to escape. When the door of opportunity opened, I killed to walk through it."

She sat frozen for several moments, stunned by his confession. What a monstrous, horrible choice to have to make—an eye for an eye. A life for a life.

Rising slowly, Kate moved on shaky legs until she was close enough to touch him. She slid her arms around his waist and rested her cheek on his chest, listened to his heart hammering as if he'd once again run miles through the rugged Afghanistan desert, eluding the enemy, struggling to survive.

"It's not your fault," she finally said.

His harsh laugh surprised her. "No one else was there, Kate. Whose fault was it?"

"The terrorists. The militants. The people who hate us. It's not like they gave you a choice."

"No." He took her arms and gently pushed her away from him. "But I have one now."

"I don't understand."

He grabbed his jeans from the chair and pulled them on, followed by his white T-shirt and boots. Grabbing his keys from the table, he looked at her. "I'm sorry. I never wanted you to know about any of that. I tried to forget it, to keep it away from you."

"It's all right. I won't melt. There's no reason to protect me."

"Maybe it was me I was protecting. I wish—"

"Joe, listen to me." She clasped her hands together, almost as if she were praying. Maybe she was. "Of course you changed. There's no way to go through that and not change. But I see you with your son. With me. You're still the same decent, honorable, heroic man and—"

"Don't say it." His eyes were haunted and filled with longing when he looked around as if memorizing every last detail before opening the door. "I'm sorry, Kate. You picked the wrong man to love."

And then he was gone.

For a long time she stared at the place he'd stood. Her cold, lonely bed was nothing compared to the empty hopelessness that swamped her now. She tried to rebuild the wall that had encased her sadness since the first time he'd walked away, but like smoke, it couldn't be controlled. Sorrow expanded inside her until it filled every part of her being and overflowed, spilling down her cheeks.

"I didn't pick you, Joe," she whispered. "My heart did."

"There's someone here to see you."

Joe looked up at his office manager. "I don't have any appointments."

Laura folded her arms over ample breasts. "You do now."

"I don't have time to see anyone today."

"Make time," she snapped, then turned and walked out.

Damn it. He had one nerve left and didn't need her or anyone else forced-marching on it. It took everything he had to show up and put in a shift, do his half of what needed doing to run the business. At night it took everything he had to keep from going to see Kate and J.T. It had been a week and he missed them like crazy. Why did this empty feeling hurt so damn much?

He loved her. That's why.

He loved her enough to stay away.

There were voices outside his office door just before an older man walked in. "Joe Morgan?"

He barely looked up. "Yeah. Look, I've got some things to do. So if you don't mind—"

"I'm Jim Robertson. Mark's father."

Joe froze on the outside while guilt moved in his chest and squeezed. Slowly he looked up, then stood and held out his hand to the balding, gray-haired man. Sad blue eyes studied him from behind wire-rimmed glasses.

"It's nice to meet you, sir."

"The pleasure is mine, son."

"Please sit down," he said, indicating one of the steel-framed, plastic-covered chairs in front of his desk.

"I don't want to take up too much of your time."

Joe rubbed the back of his neck. "My apologies. I didn't know— No offense intended, sir."

"None taken. I probably should have called before coming by."

"What can I do for you?" Besides go back in time and not get your son killed, he thought.

"I just wanted to meet you and say thanks for what you did for Mark."

"I don't understand." Joe blinked. "It's my fault he died."

"He's dead because a twisted bastard on the other side of the world hates our country and everything we stand for."

"I was the senior officer. I made the call to escape. But I didn't pay the price for failing. They made an example of Mark instead of putting the blame where it belonged."

"On you?" Jim asked.

"I survived. He didn't." Joe shrugged. "The responsibility is mine."

"It's admirable to answer for something when you're culpable. But I've talked to Mark's superior officer and the base commander made reports of the incident available to me. You risked your own life to protect an injured comrade until you were both captured. You fought to protect him until there was nothing left to fight with and tried to get him out of enemy hands." He shook his head sadly. "You're a hero, son."

"No, sir, I'm not."

"Survivor's guilt is a heavy burden to carry." Anger burned away the sorrow in Jim's eyes. "It will drag you down, crush you and destroy your life. Then the fanatic who shot my son wins again. One bullet, two kills. And that would be a damn waste."

Joe felt as if he'd just taken a punch to the gut. "I don't know what to say. If only I could have—"

"Done more?" Jim nodded. "His mother and I talk about that all the time. We encouraged him to enlist. He was drifting and needed the structure military service offers. Not a day goes by that we don't say 'if only.'"

Another father with regrets who did what he thought best, then looked back and wished he could have a do-over.

"He was a fine man," Joe said. "And an exemplary soldier. I'm proud to have served with him."

"I'm proud to have been his dad." Pride and pain mixed in the father's eyes, blending into a soul-deep grief. "And I just wanted you to know that I'm proud of you, too, son. He wrote us about you. Said you were a stand-up guy, and if he was ever in trouble you were the one to count on. I'm grateful for the opportunity to thank you in person for being with my son—" His voice broke for a moment and he swallowed. "For being with my boy when I couldn't be."

"I appreciate you saying so, sir. That means a lot to me." The fist squeezing his spirit eased. "If you don't mind my asking, how did you find me?"

"I didn't actually. Your brother found me."

"Preston?" For the second time in ten minutes Joe went still with shock.

Jim nodded. "He called and brought us—my wife and I—out from Indiana. All expenses paid. It's our first trip to Las Vegas."

"I see." That was a damn lie. He had no idea what the hell was going on.

Jim stood and held out his hand again. "If you're ever in our neck of the woods, stop by. Mary and I would like to return the hospitality."

Joe grasped the other man's palm. "I'll do that, sir."

He watched the man leave, then heard voices in the outer office. In the next second, Preston walked in.

"What the hell is going on?" Joe demanded, walking around his desk to face his brother.

"Mr. Robertson and his wife are on their way back to the hotel in the car I made available to them."

"That's not what I meant and you damn well know it. Why did you bring him here? What the hell do you think you're doing?"

"Kate called me and I called Jim. He was grateful for the chance to meet you."

So much for kicking guilt to the curb. "You think the price of a Vegas trip will buy me redemption?"

Preston stood directly in front of him. They were the same height but had never seen anything eye-to-eye. "My intention is to help a brokenhearted father find peace with losing his son. If anything had happened to you, I'd be grateful for anything, the slightest gesture of comfort anyone had to offer. If that buys *you* something it's just a happy by-product."

Joe had trouble believing his brother would have been that broken up if he hadn't come back. "There's nothing happy when you're involved. Kate had no right to bring you into this," he said through gritted teeth.

"She had every right. She loves you."

He remembered her saying it, but that was before he'd told her everything. No way could a woman like her care about a man like him now that she knew what he'd done. But Joe had no intention of discussing her with his brother.

"So tell me, Preston. What do you get out of this? The satisfaction of finding another way to screw me over?"

His brother barely flinched but never looked away. "I love you, too."

"That's hard to believe. Your definition of love is you and my wife doing the horizontal hopscotch."

Preston's blue eyes narrowed dangerously. "I'm getting sick and tired of being cast as the villain every time I clean up for you."

"If the shoe fits…"

"That's the thing, little brother. It doesn't fit. Not the way you think."

"I don't think it, I know. You're a back-stabbing bastard. Now get the hell out of my office."

Preston braced his feet wide apart. "It's time you heard my side of the story, Joe."

"I already heard all the details and it makes me sick to look at you."

"Tough." Preston stared at Joe for several moments. "She showed up at my place. Uninvited, in case you were wondering."

Joe knew the "she" in question was his ex-wife. What took hold and wouldn't let go was that it sounded like something she would have done.

"I was drunk." Preston didn't offer an explanation for why that was. It was simply a straightforward fact.

"And you think that makes it okay to sleep with my wife?"

"I have no independent recollection of sleeping with her."

"Don't go lawyer on me," Joe said.

"It has nothing to do with my profession. I don't even remember that night. Might have happened." Preston shrugged. "Might not."

"She told me everything as soon as I got off the plane."

"Her version."

Joe folded his arms over his chest. What game was he playing? "What are you talking about?"

"When you left she came to me, pretending to be lonely. I don't know what happened, but a few weeks later she claimed to be pregnant."

"But she wasn't?"

Preston laughed. "A fortuitous false positive on the pregnancy test."

"I see."

"Not yet. I'm getting to that part. I went along with her story to find out what she was up to."

"What was that?"

"Dad was right about her, Joe. She was head over heels in debt and after the Morgan man with the most money. She was hedging her bets. It turns out that because I'm a lawyer she figured I'd wind up owning all of Southwestern Helicopter."

"So that's why she told me everything as soon as I got back?"

"I insisted that if she and I had a future together we had to be honest with you. She's an opportunist, but I played the game better. There was no way you weren't going to get hurt." He blew out a long breath. "She hurried the divorce through at my insistence, then I told her it was over. You hated my guts, but at least I kept her from getting any part of the business Dad left us."

Joe studied his brother as he sifted through memories of the woman he'd married. Her coming on to him at a Vegas Valley VIP dinner. Her aggressive initiation of an affair. His father's negative opinion after that first meeting. Then his sudden orders to deploy to the Middle East. His knee-jerk proposal was half rebellion aimed at his dad and half wanting someone to come back to. He knew in his gut that she was entirely capable of the deceit Preston described. And he'd fallen for it all.

"Why didn't you tell me this sooner?" he asked.

Preston slid his hands into the pockets of his slacks. "You wouldn't have believed me, let alone admitted it was possible you'd been such a bonehead. Too busy trying to prove to Dad that your screw-up days were behind you."

Joe snorted. "We both know better than that."

"You're human."

"Do you ever get tired of being the good son?"

"I'm not always right." Preston's mouth turned up in a small smile. "I have demons, too. It's just that yours are more noble."

"Yeah. Right." Joe folded his arms over his chest.

"I always envied you, little brother."

As if he needed it, there was another shocker. "That's crazy. You were always the one voted most likely to be awesome."

Preston laughed, then turned serious. "Dad always made it a point to tell *me* how proud he was of *you*."

"That's a news flash. He never said it to me."

"I guess he couldn't. And don't ask me why. I might be awesome, but I'm not a mind reader. Maybe it was part of the military mindset."

That touched a nerve. Strong. Stoic. Silent. The description fit Joe to a *T*. It was probably training that had saved his life and might very well have cost him what made it worth living.

It had cost him Kate.

He had her to thank for bridging the gap between him and his brother. If not for her determination, Preston wouldn't be here now, telling him the truth, letting him know he'd made his father proud.

Joe held out his hand. "Thanks for bringing Mark's dad here. And for the truth."

"You're welcome." Preston ignored the hand and pulled him into a quick bear hug, then rubbed his knuckles over Joe's head the way he'd always done when they were kids.

Joe grinned. "I won't act like a damn fool again."

"Don't make any promises you can't keep." They both laughed, then Preston grew serious. "Go see Kate."

Just hearing her name made him miss her until he ached inside. "I can't."

"There you go being a damn fool."

"I'm having nightmares, Preston. I had a flashback. She was there." He ran his fingers through his hair. "I almost hurt her. There's no way I'm putting her through that."

"There's help available for post-traumatic stress disorder. And Kate doesn't strike me as the kind of woman who'd walk away when the going gets tough. She wants to help." Sympathy swirled in his brother's eyes. "Shouldn't it be her call, Joe? The only way to fail is failing to try."

"Dad used to say that."

"He was right. Talk to Kate. If I had a woman like her who cared for me the way she does for you, I wouldn't be a damn fool and let her get away."

"Understood." Joe smiled, something he wouldn't have expected. It was like getting his father's blessing. "Thanks again, bro."

"Don't call me bro. It's big brother to you," Preston said, pointing for emphasis. "And don't be a stranger."

"Count on it."

Joe sat behind his desk and for the first time let himself believe it *was* possible for him to fit in with regular people. And he had Kate to thank for getting him to this point. The problem was he'd also shut her out. Now that he was at a place where he could meet her halfway, he realized he'd been far too successful in convincing her she was better off without him.

Chapter Fifteen

Kate finally had a day off, and she'd never needed one more.

It had been over a week since the night Joe had told her what had happened to him—what he'd had to do to survive. Then he'd walked out and she hadn't heard a word from him since.

She knew this apartment which had always felt warm, cozy and inviting would forever bear painful scars and bittersweet memories of Joe. She sat on the sofa and brushed her hand over where he'd slept and smiled sadly. He was a big man and trying to get comfortable here had been an exercise in futility. Across the coffee table was the glider he'd bought to rock J.T. in. Then there was the dining table where they'd eaten together every night. As a family. Not any more.

A sob spiraled up from deep inside and lodged in her throat. "Damn. Why does it hurt so much?"

Partly because she'd seen how incredibly amazing being a family could be. Partly because she felt stupid for falling under his spell all over again. It shouldn't come as a shock that he'd left and didn't want to see her. She'd pushed. She'd gambled. She'd lost.

What surprised her was that he hadn't been by to see the baby. Or at least made arrangements to pick him up from the babysitter in order to spend time with him. There were lots of ways he could be a father without having any contact with her. But there'd been not a single word and that worried her.

As long as she lived she'd never forget the self-loathing in his eyes, the shadows that hinted at what he'd seen, what he'd been forced to do to survive, to get back home. And thank God he had. He would never be hers, but the world was a better place for him being in it. And someday she hoped he would believe that.

Maybe she should call Laura at Southwestern Helicopter. She walked to the phone on the bar and reached out a hand, then curled her fingers into her fist. How pathetic was she? His streetwise office manager would figure out in two seconds what she was doing—the equivalent of cruising by the cute guy's house to get his attention. But how else was she going to let him know that she still loved him? That she'd always love him?

What did he mean that keeping everything inside had been about protecting himself? How could he believe that she would think less of him?

Her heart ached when she remembered the last time she'd seen him, the gentle way he'd removed her hands from his body, as if he was unclean and that would rub off on her. She wanted to touch him, get through to him. Let him know that, if anything, she loved him more.

She was reaching for the phone again when it rang, startling her. Hope that it was him rushed through her only to be snuffed out when caller ID revealed her mother's number. If the baby wasn't napping, she'd have let it ring.

She picked up. "Hi, Mom."

"Hi, Katie. How are you?"

"Fine."

"Is the baby sleeping? Can you talk?" There was a tone in her mother's voice. A strain.

"Yes and yes." But probably she would only listen to the current trials and tribulations in Candy's love life. Normally that was okay with her, but she'd reached her threshold of emotional pain. Feeling as raw as she did would make it tough to bite her tongue. "Are you okay?"

"Yeah." It almost sounded like a question. "I'm a little tired, I guess."

"Bill keeping you up?"

Candy laughed. "Not the way you mean. We're taking it slow."

"So he's still around?" As soon as the words were out Kate wanted to rewind and delete.

"Amazing, isn't it?" There was just a hint of something in her mother's voice that could be sarcasm or hurt feelings. "No, I think I'm tired just because I'm getting old. Waiting tables takes more out of me now than it used to. I've got this pain in my arm. Probably pulled a muscle."

"Try a heating pad and some ibuprofen for the discomfort." Kate was grateful to change the subject.

"I'll do that as soon as I hang up." There was a pause before she said, "How's Joe?"

This was where Kate wished they were talking about her mother's life and she didn't have to share any details of her own.

"Oh, you know. Joe is Joe."

"What's wrong, Katie?"

She sighed. It was too much to hope that she could bluff her way through this. Loving him filled every fiber of her being and she wasn't a good enough actress to keep it from leaking through. Might as well come clean.

"Joe walked out over a week ago and I haven't seen him since—" The sob she'd been choking back slipped into her voice and made it break.

"Oh, baby. What happened?"

"He went through something when he was in Afghanistan, Mom." This wasn't her secret to tell and she wouldn't. "It was pretty awful and he feels like it changed him too much. That he can't be around J.T. Or me."

"That's just silly. He's a wonderful father and that child means the world to him. And you. The way he got all protective when I told him about things in the past— God knows I'm not the best judge of men, but if Joe isn't in love with you I'm the mother of the year."

Kate laughed. "Don't be so hard on yourself, Ma."

There was a deep sigh from the other end of the line. "It's a challenge not to be, sweetie. I've made so many mistakes in my life."

"And you think that makes you different from the rest of us—how?"

Instead of answering the question Candy asked, "You haven't seen Joe, but have you talked to him?"

"No."

"He hasn't called?"

"No."

"Have you called him?" When she didn't answer, her mother said, "Katie?"

"No, Mom. I haven't called him."

"Why?"

Kate sat on the floor with her back to the bar. "I don't—I can't—" She sighed. "It's just for the best."

"Because you won't be me."

"No, I—" She didn't know what to say. That was part of it.

"Kathleen Marie, don't you lie to your mother."

When Candy used both her names, Kate paid attention. "Okay. He doesn't want me the way I want him and I won't chase after him and—"

"Humiliate yourself?"

Kate winced. "I don't want to put us both in an awkward situation. A little space is probably best. For now."

"You're wrong. Little spaces get bigger until it's the damn Grand Canyon between you. Call him."

"You don't understand—"

"Excuse me. I may not have been there as much as I should have, but I'm your mother and I know you better than anyone. You're so afraid of making the same mistakes I did. Instead you're making new and different ones that are worse."

"Mom, I—"

"No, Kate. I don't want to hear it. Joe isn't perfect. He's got problems. He's human. He's also a good man. I'd be very surprised if he isn't head over heels in love with you."

"Your romantic streak is showing."

"No—" She stopped and sucked in a breath.

"Mom?"

"I'm here." She blew out a breath. "And all right. Maybe I've got romance in my soul. Enough to know that you do, too, but you're too stubborn to acknowledge it's there. I think you and Joe could have a real shot at being happy unless you refuse to take a chance and fight for him."

"He's the warrior, I'm just—" A groan on the other end stopped her. "Mom? What is it?"

There was no answer and Kate tensed. "Mom? Say something. Are you there?"

"Kate—" The single word was barely audible and filled with pain.

"Mom, what's wrong?" Adrenaline-laced anxiety pumped through her. "Tell me what's going on—"

"Pain— My arm—"

"Left arm?"

"Yes— My chest— Can't breathe—"

"Oh, God—" Kate had seen enough heart attack patients in the E.R. to know what was going on. She wanted to panic, but that wouldn't help. Struggling to keep her voice calm she said, "Mom, try to relax. I'm calling 911."

"Katie—"

"You're going to be okay." *Please, God let her be okay.* "I have to call the paramedics. I'll get help for you. Don't worry."

"Katie—"

"Hang on, Mom."

She used her cell to call the emergency number and explained the situation. The operator promised to dispatch paramedics right away. Kate hung up and paced, her mind racing. If she was right and her mother was having a heart attack, she wanted her brought to Mercy Medical instead of the small local hospital in town. The problem was that Pahrump was an hour away by ambulance, without traffic. She remembered Joe telling her about the woman in labor he'd airlifted because an accident had closed down the two-lane road.

Time was the enemy. The first sixty minutes of a trauma was the golden hour when medical intervention—doctors, drugs, equipment—could make the difference between life and death. If her mom spent that time on the road she could...

Kate bit back a sob as she speed-dialed Joe's cell number

without thinking, without hesitation. *Please God don't let him be flying.* If he was already in the chopper, he wouldn't be available.

"Come on," she breathed. "Answer, answer. Please answer the phone—"

There was cell phone static just before his voice came on. "Kate?"

"Thank God. Joe—" She choked back a sob.

"Are you okay?" Tension filled his voice. "Is something wrong with J.T.? I'll be right there—"

"No. We're fine. But I need you."

After Candy was taken by the staff from the chopper, Joe shut down power then opened the pilot's-side door and jumped down. He rounded the tail and sprinted into Mercy Medical's E.R. All he could think about was getting to Kate.

He'd been incredibly happy to hear from her until the tension and fear in her voice had come through loud and clear. Knowing her so intimately now, he understood how hard asking for help must have been. And the fact that she had called him was proof of her desperation.

He wouldn't have wished this crisis, but the words—*I need you*—were so good to hear. He hadn't dared to hope she would come to him for anything. Ever. And he was determined to be there for her. Always. No matter what.

He dashed through the automatic doors and immediately saw her pacing on the other side of the waiting room.

"Kate?"

She looked up and started toward him, then stopped in the corner by the fake ficus and lifted a hand in greeting.

He crossed the space between them in three strides and stopped in front of her. "How are you?"

"Fine. Joe, I— Thank you for getting my mom here so fast."

"I'm glad to help. Can I get you anything? Do anything?"

"No." She pushed her hair behind her ears. "J.T. is with Marilyn."

"I figured." Since she wasn't back in the trauma room, he figured she hadn't seen her mother yet and would want an update. Such as it was. "During transport your mom was conscious and alert. It's a good sign."

"Dr. Tenney wouldn't let me in the room with her," she said angrily, glancing at the double doors keeping her out. "He said I was too emotional to do either one of us any good right now."

Joe wanted badly to hold her but knew he'd blown any right to do that. "The doc's got a point. In this situation you're a daughter, not an E.R. nurse."

"Since when did you get promoted to the rank of Captain Reasonable?" she snapped.

In the next instant she looked horrified at the outburst and shocked him by bursting into tears. Turning away, she covered her face with her hands. Her shoulders shook with silent sobs and the sight tore him up inside. Without flinching, he'd faced terrorists with the flames of fanaticism burning in their eyes. But seeing her so distraught scared him spitless.

He couldn't stand to see her hurting, and it shamed him deeply that he'd caused her pain that could have been avoided if he'd simply talked to her. It sounded so easy, but not for him. What if he said something to hurt her more? Then she sniffled and he couldn't just watch. Screw the rights he'd given up.

He gently turned her and gathered her into his arms. "Everything's going to be all right. Don't cry, Katie."

She buried her face into his chest and her voice was muffled when she said, "My mom calls me th-that."

Damn. So much for saying the right thing. "I'm sorry."

"Don't be. I like it." She looked up, eyes wet, face blotchy and the most beautiful sight in the world.

"Me, too."

She brushed a finger over the front of his flight suit. "I got you all wet."

"Yeah," he said glancing down. "That's possibly the most moisture the Vegas Valley desert has seen in a long time."

"Sorry."

"Don't be," he said, echoing her words. "Are you okay?"

"Yeah." After taking a deep breath, she stepped back. A frown marred the smooth skin of her forehead. "It's just— This—my mom's attack—it was so sudden. There was no warning."

"Maybe there was."

"What do you mean?"

"The day she stopped by when you were sleeping? She mentioned a doctor's appointment. I never thought to ask about it. Why she was seeing a doctor."

"She never said a word to me about not feeling well." Her expression was bleak. "Because she didn't want to hear the scolding speech from me. I'm so judgmental. When we were on the phone I said something sarcastic about the new guy in her life. Then she gave me a lecture about—" Her lips quivered before she blew out a breath and struggled for control. "I was glad she changed the subject to the pain in her arm. I told her to try a heating pad and painkiller. That'll show her heart who's boss—"

"Stop it, Kate."

"What if I never get the chance to tell her I'm sorry?"

He curved his fingers around her upper arms. "Beating yourself up is self-destructive and a waste of energy. It doesn't do you or your mom a damn bit of good. Whatever happens, we'll deal with it."

She stared at him as if he'd grown another head. Maybe he had. Thanks to her he was thinking clearly for the first time in longer than he could remember. The important stuff was as clear to him as the view of the Vegas Valley mountains when the wind blew out the haze. He wanted Kate more than anything in the world. Now all he had to do was figure out how to make it happen.

After bringing two cups of vending-machine coffee, Joe sat beside Kate in the waiting room and took her hand in his. It was a good sign that she didn't pull away. Finally the doctor came through the double doors. Mitch Tenney was about Joe's height with dark hair and eyes. Everything about him was dark, including the five o'clock shadow on his jaw. He was sensitive as a pit bull, but if you had a medical emergency he was the guy you wanted in your corner.

"How's my mother?" Kate asked, on her feet as soon as she saw him.

"Stable." Mitch looked down at her. "The cardiac enzymes are elevated. It's a heart attack, but swift intervention minimized damage to the muscle."

"Is she going to be okay?" Kate asked.

"It looks good." His glance skipped between them. "Thanks to G.I. Joe and the magic helicopter."

Kate's shoulders relaxed. "Thank God."

"He had nothing to do with it," the doctor said. He also had a reputation for brutal honesty. "And your mother's been warned. She needs to start taking care of herself."

"I'll see that she does," Kate promised.

"Good luck with that." The tone was cynical, a clear indication, thought Joe, that this guy didn't know how incredibly stubborn his E.R. nurse could be when she was determined to get her way.

If she weren't, she would have given up on him when he'd walked out on her the first time. He wouldn't make that mistake again.

"When can I see her?" Kate asked.

"Right now she wouldn't know you from a palm tree. We gave her something for pain and to help her rest. She's going to CCU in a few minutes. You can see her there."

Without another word he walked away.

"Dr. Sunshine," Joe said wryly.

"Yeah. But he's right. And sometimes we shouldn't get a spoonful of sugar to help the medicine go down because a dose of reality is just what the doctor ordered," she said. Then she met his gaze and sighed. "Thanks for staying."

When she started to move away, he put his hand on her arm. "Katie, wait—"

"Let me go, Joe. I really appreciate that you were here, but the truth is, it's just too hard to see you and—" She shook her head.

"Okay." He blew out a breath. "I deserve that. But there's something I thought you should know."

"What?"

"I talked to Preston and you were right." He blew out a long breath. "There *was* another side to the story. There was no affair and he had a good reason for everything he did."

"I'm glad. J.T. should have a relationship with his uncle. Thanks for letting me know."

He cut off her escape route when she was going to walk past him. "There's more. And if you still want to walk away after I say what I need to, then I won't stop you."

"I can't. I—" She looked away for a moment, then said, "I just don't have any reserves left."

"You're probably the strongest woman I've ever known. I'm very sorry your mother is here, but I can't be sorry that I have this chance to talk to you."

"Why now? It's not—" She shook her head.

"You don't have to do anything but listen while I explain." When she finally nodded, he let out the breath he'd been holding. "I'm an idiot."

"If you're waiting for me to argue with that, it'll be a cold day in hell." One corner of her mouth curved up.

"Okay. I deserve that. The thing is I broke things off the first time because I was afraid of losing you while I was gone overseas."

"Yeah. I figured that out."

He should have known. "Then I was on borrowed time with you because I came back with wounds in places that no one could see. No one except you."

"I was never afraid of you, Joe. You'd never hurt me. All I wanted to do was help."

"I understand that now." He rubbed a hand across the back of his neck. "I just didn't believe I could be normal and give you the life you deserve."

"All I wanted was you," she said.

Past tense. God, he hoped he could give them a chance in the present and make a future. "I've always been drawn to risk, to thrills. The adrenaline rush of danger. That never gave me pause because I didn't have anything to lose. Until I fell in love with you."

Her gaze jumped to his, surprise replacing the bruised expression just for a moment. "Shutting me out is a funny way of showing it."

"I couldn't let you see inside me. I couldn't chance that the ugliness would push you away."

"So you just pushed me away and made it a sure thing." She shook her head. "I appreciate you explaining things, Joe. I really do. But I'm not sure— I don't think we can get back what we had before—"

"You're wrong. Somewhere I heard that you can't build a life on memories. I know for a fact that's not true. If not for memories, I'd have no life." He reached in his back pocket and pulled out his wallet, plucking a tattered envelope from it. "Here."

She took it, careful not to touch him. After looking for a moment, she met his gaze, shock and awe in her eyes. "This is my letter."

"Yeah."

"The letter I sent telling you I was pregnant with J.T."

"I know."

She met his gaze. "You kept it all this time?"

"It arrived just before that last mission and I stuck it in my pocket. When the bad guys were closing in on us, I hid it in my boot. The whole time they held me, I read it over and over. I remembered you and me. It saved my life. I kept going so I could come back and tell you I love you. I always have, from the first moment I saw you. You're my heart, my soul. You're everything—" Intensity hummed through him. "Tell me that's not enough to build a life on."

"I—I don't know what to say."

"That's okay. I'll do the talking. It's long overdue. If you believe anything, believe this." He took her hands in his and held on tight. "I swear I'll never let you down. You said you love me. I'm hoping you still do, in spite of the stupid way I handled everything. If you give me another chance, I'll spend the rest of my life proving to you that I'm worth it."

For the second time that day, tears welled in her eyes and he hoped these were the happy kind.

"You don't have to prove anything to me, Joe. I've always known you were worth it." She reached up and cupped his cheek in her hand. "I loved you the first time I saw you in the E.R. and I love you now. I don't think I have it in me to stop loving you."

He cupped her hand with his own, then turned his lips into it and placed a kiss in her palm.

When she nestled against him and slid her arms around his waist, he had no choice but to kiss the living daylights out of her. How fitting that they stood a few feet from where he had seen her for the first time—a short distance from where he'd fallen in love with her forever.

When they finally came up for air, he looked into her eyes. "Since I crashed and burned the first time I asked you to marry me just around the corner from where we are now, I should hold off and dazzle you with romance and flowers, just to make sure the odds are in my favor."

"Okay."

"But as a man of action, waiting doesn't wash. Will you marry me, Kate?"

Her eyes were almost green, as if the sun was shining from the inside out of her. "The last thing my mother said before her attack was that I need to stop worrying so much about making a mistake."

"I know this communication thing is new and different for me, but I can't tell. Was that a yes?"

"Oh, yeah." She smiled and flashed him her dimples. "That was a definite, emphatic yes."

"There is a God." He let out a big breath and grinned down at her. "And someday maybe I'll figure out what I've done to deserve you."

"You're a hero—"

He shook his head. "I'm just a man trying to do the right thing."

"That's what a hero is, big guy."

"If you say so. It seems appropriate that you agreed to be my wife here in Mercy Medical Center where the real heroes are. Whether or not I belong, I'm just grateful you said yes."

"I said yes because I love you." She stood on tiptoe and kissed the scar on his chin. "And I know how to hang on tight when a hero comes along."

* * * * *

Love Inspired
HISTORICAL

*Powerful, engaging stories of romance, adventure and
faith set in the past—when life was simpler and
faith played a major role in everyday lives.*

See below for a sneak preview of
HIGH COUNTRY BRIDE
by Jillian Hart

*Love Inspired Historical—love and faith
throughout the ages*

Silence remained between them, and she felt the rake of his gaze, taking her in from the top of her wind-blown hair where escaped tendrils snapped in the wind to the toe of her scuffed, patched shoes. She watched him fist up his big, work-roughened hands and expected the worst.

"You never told me, Miz Nelson. Where are you going to go?" His tone was flat, his jaw tensed as if he were still fighting his temper. His blue gaze shot past her to watch the children going about their picking up.

"I don't know." Her throat went dry. Her tongue felt thick as she answered. "When I find employment, I could wire a payment to you. Rent. Y-you aren't think-ing of bringing the sher-iff in?"

"You think I want *payment?*" He boomed like winter thunder. *"You think I want rent money?"*

"Frankly, I don't know what you want."

"I'll tell you what I don't want. I don't want—" His words cannoned in the silence as he paused, and a passing pair of geese overhead honked in flat-noted tones. He grimaced, and it was impossible to know what he would say or do.

She trembled, not from fear of him, she truly didn't believe he would strike her, but from the unknown. Of being forced to take the frightening step off the only safe spot she'd known since she'd lost Pa's house.

When you were homeless, everything seemed so fragile, so easily off balance, for it was a big, unkind world for a woman alone with her children. She had no one to protect her. No one to care. The truth was, she'd never had those things in her husband. How could she expect them from any stranger? Especially this man she hardly knew, who was harsh and cold and hardhearted.

And, worse, what if he brought in the law?

"You can't keep living out of a wagon," he said, still angry, the cords still straining in his neck. "Animals have enough sense to keep their young cared for and safe."

Yes, it was as she'd thought. He intended to be as cruel about this as he could be. She spun on her heel, pulling up all her defenses, and was determined to let his upcoming hurtful words roll off her like rainwater on an oiled tarp. She grabbed the towel the children had neatly folded and tossed it into the laundry box in the back of the wagon.

"Miz Nelson. I'm talking to you."

"Yes, I know. If you expect me to stand there while you tongue lash me, you're mistaken. I have packing to get to." Her fingers were clumsy as she hefted the bucket of water she'd brought for washing—she wouldn't need that now—and heaved.

His hand clasped on the handle beside hers, and she could feel the life and power of him vibrate along the thin metal. "Give it to me."

Her fingers let go. She felt stunned as he walked away, easily carrying the bucket that had been so heavy to her, and quietly, methodically, put out the small cooking fire. He did not seem as ominous or as intimidating—somehow—as he stood in the shadows, bent to his task, although she couldn't say why that was. Perhaps it was because he wasn't acting the way she was used to men acting. She was quite used to doing all the work.

Jamie scurried over, juggling his wooden horses, to watch. Daisy hung back, eyes wide and still, taking in the mysterious goings-on.

He is different when he's near to them, she realized. He didn't seem harsh, and there was no hint of anger—or, come to think of it, any other emotion—as he shook out the empty bucket, nodded once to the children and then retraced his path to her.

"Let me guess." He dropped the bucket onto the tailgate, and his anger appeared to be back. Cords strained in his neck and jaw as he growled at her. "If you leave here, you don't know where you're going and you have no money to get there with?"

She nodded. "Yes, sir."

"Then get you and your kids into the wagon. I'll hitch up your horses for you." His eyes were cold and yet they were not unfeeling as he fastened his gaze on hers. "I have an empty shanty out back of my house that no one's living in. You can stay there for the night."

"What?" She stumbled back, and the solid wood of the tailgate bit into the small of her back. "But—"

"There will be no argument," he bit out, interrupting her. "None at all. I buried a wife and son years ago, what was most precious to me, and to see you and them neglected like this—with no one to care—" His jaw ground again and his eyes were no longer cold.

Joanna didn't think she'd ever seen anything sadder than Aiden McKaslin as the sun went down on him.

* * * * *

Don't miss this deeply moving story,
HIGH COUNTRY BRIDE,
available July 2008
from the new Love Inspired Historical line.

Also look for SEASIDE CINDERELLA
by Anna Schmidt,
where a poor servant girl and a wealthy merchant
prince might somehow make a life together.

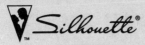

Romantic
SUSPENSE

**Sparked by Danger,
Fueled by Passion.**

Conard County: The Next Generation

When he learns the truth about his father, military man Ethan Parish is determined to reunite with his long-lost family in Wyoming. On his way into town, he clashes with policewoman Connie Halloran, whose captivating beauty entices him. When Connie's daughter is threatened, Ethan must use his military skills to keep her safe. Together they race against time to find the little girl and confront the dangers inherent in family secrets.

Look for

A Soldier's Homecoming

**by *New York Times*
bestselling author**

Rachel Lee

Available in July wherever you buy books.

REQUEST YOUR FREE BOOKS!

2 FREE NOVELS PLUS 2 FREE GIFTS!

 Silhouette®

SPECIAL EDITION®

Life, Love and Family!

YES! Please send me 2 FREE Silhouette Speāal Edition® novels and my 2 FREE gifts (gifts are worth about $10). After receiving them, if I don't wish to receive any more books, I can return the shipping statement marked "cancel." If I don't cancel, I will receive 6 brand-new novels every month and be billed just $4.24 per book in the U.S. or $4.99 per book in Canada, plus 25¢ shipping and handling per book and applicable taxes, if any*. That's a savings of at least 15% off the cover price! I understand that accepting the 2 free books and gifts places me under no obligation to buy anything. I can always return a shipment and cancel at any time. Even if I never buy another book from Silhouette, the two free books and gifts are mine to keep forever.

235 SDN EEYU 335 SDN EEY6

Name _____ (PLEASE PRINT) _____

Address _____ Apt. # _____

City _____ State/Prov. _____ Zip/Postal Code _____

Signature (if under 18, a parent or guardian must sign)

Mail to the **Silhouette Reader Service:**
IN U.S.A.: P.O. Box 1867, Buffalo, NY 14240-1867
IN CANADA: P.O. Box 609, Fort Erie, Ontario L2A 5X3
Not valid to current subscribers of Silhouette Speāal Edition books.

Want to try two free books from another line?
Call 1-800-873-8635 or visit www.morefreebooks.com.

* Terms and prices subject to change without notice. N.Y. residents add applicable sales tax. Canadian residents will be charged applicable provināal taxes and GST. This offer is limited to one order per household. All orders subject to approval. Credit or debit balances in a customer's account(s) may be offset by any other outstanding balance owed by or to the customer. Please allow 4 to 6 weeks for delivery. Offer available while quantities last.

Your Privacy: Silhouette is committed to protecting your privacy. Our Privacy Policy is available online at www.eHarlequin.com or upon request from the Reader Service. From time to time we make our lists of customers available to reputable third parties who may have a product or service of interest to you. If you would prefer we not share your name and address, please check here. ☐

SSE08

HIGH-SOCIETY SECRET PREGNANCY

Park Avenue Scandals

Self-made millionaire Max Rolland had given
up on love until he meets socialite fundraiser
Julia Prentice. After their encounter Julia finds
herself pregnant, but a mysterious blackmailer
threatens to use this surprise pregnancy and ruin
his reputation. Max must decide whether to turn
his back on the woman carrying his child or risk
everything, including his heart....

**Don't miss the next installment of
the Park Avenue Scandals series—
Front Page Engagement
by Laura Wright—
coming in August 2008
from Silhouette Desire!**

Always Powerful, Passionate and Provocative.

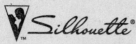

COMING NEXT MONTH

SSECNM0608